The Penny Red Enigma

The Penny Red Enigma

Printed and Bound by Gorham Printing
   Rochester, Washington

Published by Hal Burton Publishing
   Lilliwaup, Washington

First Edition, First Printing – July 2004

South Dakota prairie photo - courtesy Harold Ferguson family

Author's photo – by Sarah Granberg

Map of Haakon & Stanley County- courtesy of Karyl Sandal
   Register of Deeds, Haakon County, South Dakota

Cover design by Jeanette Burton

Epilogue Poem, *My Harvest Song*, Gregory Burton
   Copyright © 2004, by Gregory Burton

Library of Congress Control Number: 2004092699

ISBN – 0-9725707-4-8

The Penny Red Enigma

Hal Burton

Acknowledgements

This book could never have been written without the help of many people. There are five individuals and one group, however, that made significant contributions to this published version. Ilene Breen read the first draft and got me started in the right direction. Gert Williams read the second draft and her inputs and suggestions were extremely helpful. Greg Burton and Jerry Horstman were my two diligent editors, and thank goodness. I owe both of them many thanks for their hours of work. During the time of the final rewrite, I began participating in the *Olympic Poets and Writers Workshop*, in Shelton, Washington, and I thank this group for their timely feedback.

Most of all I couldn't have even finished the first draft, let alone the final version without the assistance of my wife, Jeanette Burton. Her story line ideas and especially her insights regarding rural South Dakota were invaluable.

Part One

"If a man curses his father or mother, his lamp will be snuffed out in pitch darkness."

"An inheritance quickly gained at the beginning will not be blessed at the end."

Proverbs 20:20-21

Who They Are

Giles Duncombe – London businessman and family patriarch
Margaret Duncombe – Giles' first wife
Esther Duncombe – Giles' second wife
George & Ethel Smythe - Duncombe Servants
Malcolm Jones - Barrister

Giles Duncombe Jr. – Giles & Margaret's oldest child
Ruth Duncombe – Wife of Giles Jr.
James Duncombe – Second eldest son
Terrance Duncombe – Third eldest son
Evelyn Duncombe – Wife of Terrance
Mary Duncombe Kirkland – Daughter of Giles & Margaret
Tyler Kirkland – Mary's husband
William Duncombe – Youngest Son

Edward Keith – Friend of William Duncombe
Ethel Prentise – William's house cleaner
Oren Eflow – Private Investigator
Wendell Eflow - Investigator
Angus Tetherton - Investigator
Lenora Franklin – Cousin of Edward Keith
Anne Spencer - London Seamstress
Martha Franklin – Lenora's sister
Michael O'Toole – New York dock worker
Jesse Mason – Lila's husband

The Children

Michael Duncombe - Son of Giles Duncombe Jr.
Sarah Duncombe – Daughter of Giles Duncombe Jr.
Stephen Duncombe – Son of Terrance Duncombe
Olivia Kirkland – Daughter of Mary Duncombe Kirkland
Henry Spencer – Son of Anne Spencer
Lila Mason – Daughter of Lenora

Prologue

Giles Duncombe was thirty-seven years old when England gave birth to the world's first postage stamps. From that day in 1840 onward, the design of the one-penny value postage stamp was regarded as perfection itself.

The Penny Black and later the Penny Red stamps bore letters in their corners, alphabetically indicating their position on the printed sheet. This network of lettered squares was designed for the sheet of 240 individual stamps. The Postal authorities believed this arrangement provided one means of protecting against forgeries.

An enigma resulted from these precautions. People began to save the used stamps to try to reconstruct the sheet of 240.

Multiple engraved plates for each design were required for the volume demands of the mid-nineteenth century. The One-Penny of this period was printed from plates #71 through #225, each with the engraved likeness of Queen Victoria and with position letters in all four corners. The sheet of 240 images was printed in red ink.

British Isles

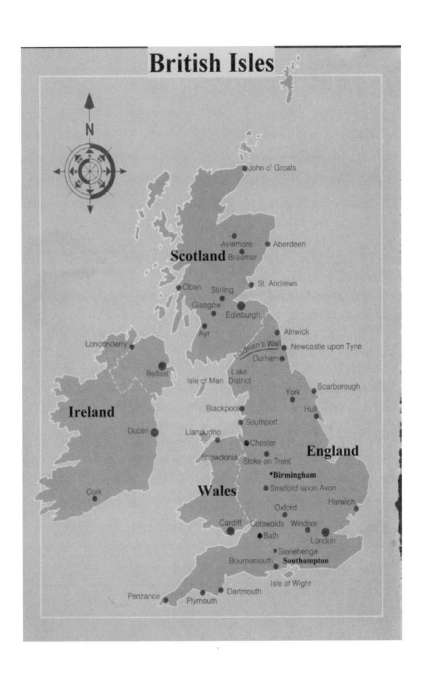

Chapter One

The gaslights in the small room burned brighter than those in the rest of the shop and cast two shadows eerily on the whitewashed brick wall. It was half-past eight in the evening and the lamps over the printing press in the main production room were turned low, as they had been the previous two nights.

Henry Farnsworth was nearly finished cleaning the plate he had painstakingly engraved with the words given to him by Mr. Duncombe two nights beforehand. Duncombe, hovering near, adjusted his Pince-nez eyeglasses for a better view.

"How much longer?" he asked, trying not to sound impatient.

"I'm about finished, but I have to complete setting up the small press and that will take a few minutes," Farnsworth answered.

"I'll go back to my office then and get the sheet," Giles Duncombe said.

When Duncombe returned, the master printer for Derkins, Falcon and Duncombe had the new plate in the press. He reached out to get the sheet from his superior. Henry didn't understand what Duncombe's motives were, but the ten Pounds he was being paid more than quelled his curiosity. He also knew that if the Post Office authorities found out what they were doing, he, Mr. Duncombe and the firm would be in serious trouble. He secured the new plate and then aligned the sheet originally printed from plate #225. The newly engraved words would be printed on the reverse side of thirty stamps of the already printed sheet of 240 stamps. The first Penny postage labels had been black, but the cancellations in black ink didn't show, so the penny value color was changed to red in 1841.

"All ready," he said to Duncombe.

It took only a few seconds to print the one sheet.

"As soon as the ink dries, I'll put it through the perforator, apply the adhesive and then you can have the sheet."

"You'll destroy this new plate?"

Henry knew it really wasn't a question, but nodded anyway.

"You are a good employee and friend, Henry." Giles coughed. Then a second time, more deeply. Then regaining his composure, he continued.

"I appreciate your cooperation and silence in this matter. I'm sure you realize the risks and the penalties if what we've done is ever found out."

Henry nodded.

"Very well, here is an additional five pounds. I'll leave you to do the clean up, and I trust you'll have a pleasant Sunday. Goodnight."

When Henry finished cleaning the press he set about breaking up the steel plate into small pieces. He thought to himself. *What a waste to destroy what he'd spent so much time on.* Next, he returned plate 225 to its case. He had been the master engraver at Dirken's since sixty-eight and for the past two years was supervising the engraving and printing of England's postage stamps. He extinguished the lamps and put on his coat. He was glad this job was done, but the extra five Pounds had been a pleasant surprise.

The Duncombe residence on High Street was built in the Queen Anne style of the 18th century. Giles at first hated the idea of a red brick exterior, but Esther explained that this style was having a popular resurgence as opposed to the more contemporary baroque look. Her friends had insisted that manor houses built by the architect Richard Tellson were in vogue. He eventually capitulated to his new wife and Tellson was hired.

Giles Duncombe climbed the stairs to his room. It took more effort than he felt like expending at the late hour. George had offered to help him, but he declined and told George to retire for the night after he put their hansom cab away. *Thank goodness George was waiting for him at the shop*, he thought. The cool London night air made his breathing even more difficult. After disrobing, Giles put the sheet of 240 stamps in his wall safe. He pulled on his nightcap, blew out the candles and said aloud, "Finally done."

This part of the plan was complete and now he could await death with some satisfaction knowing that his strategy would bring his family together. If not while he lived, at least thereafter. He thought about the five of them as he lay waiting for sleep to take over and give his hurting body a much-needed rest.

Giles, Jr. The eldest. He hadn't spoken to Giles in two years and he gathered from James that Giles had not seen Terrance, William or Mary in that time either. Giles Jr. lives in York with his wife Ruth and their children Michael and Sarah. He teaches literature at York University.

James. Only he and William still regarded their father with favor. James joined the firm in sixty-one. Still single, James lives alone in London.

Terrance. At thirty-one, Terrance resides comfortably with his wife Evelyn and son Stephen in Bath. Terrance occasionally sees William, but not his other brothers or sister. His publishing business regularly takes him to London.

Mary. Now Mrs. Tyler Kirkland, Mary lives in Birmingham where Tyler owns a small woolen mill. She hasn't seen her father in two years, but he knows she gets family information through William. They have a daughter, Olivia.

William. The youngest at twenty-six, lives in Bath. In Terrance's last letter, he mentioned he hadn't seen William in some time. He also commented on William's latest romance with a young librarian. He remembered her first name as Lenora. He hoped the difference in their class would be apparent and soon cool his brother's passion.

What a mess, Giles mused. Then his thoughts shifted to Esther. Esther, his second wife died just four month ago. *So soon.* He heard Jenny in the hall, *probably turning down the lamps*. It was late. Tomorrow he had much to do.

The further they traveled the rougher the ride became. The once smooth cobble stone surface changed first to uneven ruts and finally to what was only a two-wheel dirt path. *George will have to take the cab to the Wheelwright for repairs soon*, Giles thought. The ride smoothed out once again as they neared Balmouth. Malcolm Jones' office in Balmouth was two hours away from London, and despite the bad road and heavy carriage traffic, George made good time and they arrived just before ten. *Not the 15 mph advertised by Forder & Co., but considering the road conditions, not too bad,* thought Giles.

Malcolm had been his barrister for as long as Giles could remember. They met at Eldon College, near Balmouth.

Malcolm's firm now had offices in London and Balmouth, but he had long since given up his rooms in London and opted for the quieter country life, only going to London when necessary. The London office represented the Duncombe Shipping interests but when Giles had personnel needs, they usually met in Balmouth.

"George, I'll be at least an hour," Giles said.

"Yes Sir. I'll have lunch at the Ox Bow and be back at half past twelve to see if you're ready, if that's all right?"

"Make it one. That should give us both enough time," Giles responded.

Malcolm rose as his clerk Thomas showed Giles into his private office. Giles looked tired and distraught. His face more drawn than when they last met. *Most likely the long ride*, thought Malcolm. He smiled, walked around the desk and offered his hand.

"Good morning Giles." Unlike Giles, Malcolm always had a jocund disposition in the morning, plus he was eager to discuss the contents of the letter Giles had sent.

"And to you, my friend," Giles said, now more animated.

"Sit, please. Some tea?"

He took Giles' coat and bowler and hung them on the stand behind his walnut, double-face desk.

Giles nodded. "Yes, thanks." Malcolm poured the tea.

"All right then. Your letter was vague, to say the least. I appreciate the fact that you like intrigue and once reveled in organizing treasure hunts when we were students at Eldon, but I gather this is no frivolous treasure hunt. Especially for you to travel here rather than wait till I'm in London next week. What's so serious that you dreamed up this wild idea involving your children who, I might add, are a bit too old for game playing?"

Giles was silent, so Malcolm continued.

"Why don't you start at the beginning."

"Malcolm, I'm dying. The doctors say I have a month, maybe two at best."

"My god Giles, how long have you known?" Malcolm rose and started toward Giles.

Giles raised his hand. "No, no, that's fine. I've known for several weeks. You're the first person other than my doctor to know."

"The children don't?" he said incredulously.

"No. Most of them don't even talk to each other, let alone their father. That is why you must help me put my plan, with the intrigue you suggest, into action."

George Smythe finished his Shepherd's Pie and ordered another pint of bitter. That's one thing he liked about the occasional trips to Balmouth. The Ox Bow had excellent Shepherd's Pie and it was only two pence a slice.

George had been with the Duncombe family nineteen years now. He and his wife, Jenny, were hired together back in fifty-two when the first Mrs. Duncombe ran the household. There'd been a third staff member then, because except for Giles Jr. away at Eldon, the children were all at home. The maid, Mrs. Willowby, left the household in sixty-nine when Sr. married Esther Lassiter.

George checked his pocket watch. *Just enough time to finish this pint and get back to the barrister's office. Sr., as he referred to Giles privately, had sure been acting strangely of late. Three nights in a row George took him to the printing office, two days to his doctor, and now this trip to Balmouth.*

"Giles, this is preposterous! Why go to all this trouble?"

Giles sat, unmoving, as Malcolm continued.

"I realize that before Margaret's illness and death your family was very close. And I appreciate that some of the children have never accepted Esther. I was there, remember, when Giles Jr. and James had that fight over the business, but this, it's bizarre!"

"Nevertheless, it's what I intend to do, with or without your help," Giles said, his tone unyielding. He rose with some effort and pulled a handkerchief from his jacket sleeve, just in time to cover his mouth when he coughed.

Malcolm slumped in his chair. "Very well, my friend. Give me the letters. I'll revise your will and have a copy for you to approve next week at the London office."

George was waiting for him as expected. As he climbed into the cab he thought, *almost finished.*

Tomorrow the final part of his plan would be set in motion. He tapped on the roof of the cab. "Let's go home George."

The *District* line opened the previous year so now if you got off at Westminster Bridge, you could connect to the *Metropolitan* line. The Metro, as Londoner's called it, stopped at Gloucester Road and Giles' bank was just a block from the above ground entrance. Giles liked to ride the new underground rail system even though some of the twelve-seat carriages often were overcrowded. Once he'd been riding through the Tower Hill tunnel when the steam engine-driven lift broke down. He didn't like the experience and told his friend James Greatland as much, when he next saw him at their club. James' firm engineered and built the tunnel that went from Tower Hill to Vine Lane, the stop just before Gloucester. James told Giles many times that he should be proud to ride on the very first tube railway in the world.

He arrived at the bank a few minutes early, but spotted Brambly as he entered.

"Good morning Mr. Brambly." Giles extended his hand.

"I appreciate you setting aside time for me on such short notice." He smoothed down his thinning gray hair, unbuttoned his coat and took a seat across from the banker.

William Brambly was a little taken aback. Giles Duncombe was one of his largest depositors and setting time aside, as Duncombe put it, gave him great pleasure.

"Of course, Mr. Duncombe, this bank always has time for you." Then, trying not to sound too solicitous: "How may I help you?"

Five minutes later, Brambly wished he'd never asked the question of Giles Duncombe.

"The whole amount?" Brambly stared at Giles in disbelief.

"Yes, the amount indicated on that paper and signed by myself. You'll note my barrister in Balmouth witnessed it, and I want the bank draft ready to pick up no later than ten o'clock, two days hence."

"But this is only 100 pounds short of your total balance."

"I am aware of that, Sir," Giles responded, rising to leave.

"And, oh yes, I trust that word of this transaction will not leave your person."

Brambly nodded, still not having fully recovered his composure.

"Very well then, my man George and I will be here promptly at ten." Giles turned to go and then, almost as an afterthought, turned back.

"William." Brambly was surprised, as in all the years Giles Duncombe had dealt with him he had never used his given name.

"Yes," Brambly said, rising and showing his pleasure at the familiarity.

Giles reached across the desk and took Brambly's hand.

"Really, I thank you. I appreciate how this looks and I will expect your confidentiality."

Then, turning away again, "Goodbye."

William Brambly sat still for a moment. He couldn't get over Duncombe's instructions. He rose and called to one of his assistants.

"Gerald, come here please."

Brambly explained his needs, leaving out the specifics of Duncombe's involvement.

Gerald looked at his supervisor in disbelief. "By ten on Thursday?"

Giles got back to his office just after noon. His plans were just about complete. He did a few odd tasks, selected one of his favorite books of poems from his bookcase, and told Hester, his secretary, that he was leaving for lunch at his club.

The walk up the stairs from the tube station and then to his office had tired him more that he realized. By the time he got to the club, he wished he'd gone home instead. However, the club was warm and comforting and he soon felt much better. *I'll read for a while.*

A waiter approached. Giles tried to remember his name. *Alfred*, he thought.

"Afternoon, Mr. Duncombe."

"A brandy, please." Then hesitantly he added, "Alfred."

"Thank you sir, right away."

Giles opened the poem book to one of his favorites, *The Invictus,* by William Henley. Soon, however, his thoughts once again returned to his plan for uniting the family. He set the book down.

Would it work? Was it too much?

The children had always liked their guessing games and secret treasure hunts when they were little. He remembered the last time they all went to York. William was just five. Giles Jr., at sixteen, announced he was too old for their annual family vacation and treasure hunt. Once they got to the old family farm, however, he seemed to be just as enthusiastic as in previous years. That was their last trip as a family. Eighteen-Fifty. A lifetime ago.

The Invictus

William Ernest Henley

Out of the night that covers me,
Black as a Pit from pole to pole,
I thank whatever gods may be
For my unconquerable soul.

In the fell clutch of circumstance
I have not winced nor cried aloud,
Under the bludgeonings of chance
My head is bloody, but unbowed.

Beyond this place of wrath and tears
Looms but the horror of the shade,
And yet the menace of the years
Finds, and shall find me, unafraid.

It matters not how straight the gate,
How charged with punishments the scroll,
I am the master of my fate:
I am the captain of my soul.

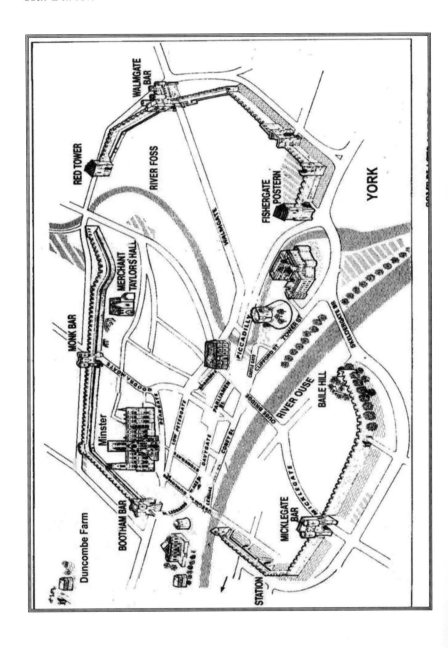

Chapter Two

1850

The family farm was north of York, near one of the oldest fragments of the original Roman wall and just west of Bootham Bar. Adjacent was the family burial grounds. Giles Sr. had traced the Duncombe line back to the early 17th century and most of the Duncombes were buried in the cemetery. More recent ancestors, however, were interred in the near-by-family mausoleum, built in 1829 after the Ouse River spilled over its banks in 1828 and flooded the cemetery. When the children were young, they called the mausoleum their "home of death."

The only people living at the farm in 1850 were the caretaker and his wife, Jasper and Edythe Fitzworth. They resided in a small bungalow near the main house.

The two-hour ride from Charing Cross Station had been tiring. The children, especially the youngest, William and Mary, kept Margaret busy. All were exhausted and hungry when they pulled into York station, so Jasper and the coach were a welcome sight. As they neared the house they were also welcomed by smells emanating from the kitchen of a scrumptious turkey dinner prepared by Edythe. They all ate voraciously. Margaret and Giles stayed up for a while after the children were in bed to discuss final plans for the treasure hunt.

By noon mealtime the next day, the older children were beginning to pester their parents as to when the treasure hunt would begin. Even Giles Jr., whom earlier had been so vocal about the childishness of it all, joined in the query. James and Terrance were especially keen to get started, as the "treasure" was usually small gifts for each child and plenty of sweet treats. William too jumped about excitedly, emulating his siblings even though he had little idea what they meant by a treasure hunt. When Mary also joined ranks, Giles laughed and relented.

"All right, all right," he said.

"Tomorrow after breakfast we will start." He knew he still had some work to do. As he and Margaret had discussed, they'd just about run out of places to hide things. The older children were a lot smarter too, and his riddles had to be more challenging each year.

"So, have your outdoors clothes on. We shall start promptly at nine o'clock."

Giles had done some preliminary work and he used the remainder of the day to finish hiding the balance of the clues. This proved to be no easy task. Either Giles Jr., Terrance or Mary seemed to materialize out of nowhere to observe his every move. Finally, just before supper, he finished.

"Father," James called, as soon as he washed after breakfast. "We're ready."

"All right then. Here is your first clue. Remember, Will and Mary must be included. Work as a team and stay together."

They all gathered around James as he read the first clue.

"A planter holds the key."

"So begin at trails end and follow me."

James turned toward his father, but he was already walking away.

"Father," James called. "This is hard. What trail?"

"I have an idea," Giles Jr. said. "Follow me."

And they were off. Mary took William's hand and hurried to catch up.

As Giles had guessed, the "trail" in the riddle was the path that led from the back of the caretaker's house, down to the bank of the river. At the front of their dock, Margaret had a huge planter box filled with spring and summer bloomers.

"Here," Giles shouted. "It's got to be here."

"In the box?" Terrance exclaimed.

"I don't know for sure. Stop chattering and start digging around."

Mary, who had just caught up, let loose of William's hand and started digging in the box too.

"Careful not to ruin Mother's flowers," said Terrance.

"Nothing here!" James, always the Gloomy Gus, rose and turned to his brother. "This must be wrong."

"No, it's got to be here." Then suddenly, remembering Terrance's admonition. "Wait, maybe it's under the box. James, give me a hand."

The two of them, with some effort, pushed the box aside and there beneath lay a metal container in a freshly dug hole.

"See, it is here," said a vindicated Giles. He reached in and removed the tin, handing it to James.

James opened the box, unfolded the paper and read the second clue aloud.

"The age of crowning, plus a three."

"Takes you west to a sunshade tree."

Giles scanned the perimeter.

"There's trees all around. Maple, some oak and some elms," he said.

William, not knowing what was really going on, but nevertheless enjoying the game, tugged on Mary's hand.

"Go, go," he cried.

Giles sat down and reread the clue. Rising, he handed the paper to Terrance, who passed it on to James, who was equally puzzled.

"All right. It's obvious to me that we are to go west to one of those trees," Giles said. He continued. "But, between here and any of those trees to the west, there's a lot of choices."

"How do we know which way is west?" asked Mary.

"Oh, come on Mary," said Terrance. "The sun comes up in the east and sets in the west, so it has to be that way."

Terrance pointed toward the line of elms that bordered the road. Mary stuck out her tongue.

Giles had been quiet, but now walked over to James and took the paper.

"Any ideas, James?" He started to speak when Terrance interrupted.

"What's *crowning* mean? That's got to be a big clue," he said.

Suddenly Giles clapped his hands. "That's it," he said.

"The age of crowning."

They all looked at him in puzzlement. Even William seemed to have a look of bewilderment.

"It's really simple. You see, he's got to be referring to Queen Victoria's crowning." He continued in spite of their looks of doubt.

"Let's see. James, she was eighteen, wasn't she?" Giles said.

"Yes, eighteen," Terrance said before James could answer.

"So," Giles said, "eighteen plus three is twenty-one."

"That must mean that the next clue is by one of those elm trees," Giles continued.

"Which one?" James asked impatiently.

"Just let me finish," said Giles. "The twenty-one likely means twenty-one paces, or yards, but I'm betting paces."

Then pointing. "And that's about due west. Come on, let's go!"

Giles led the way, carefully counting his strides. "One, two, three, -----."

At the end of twenty-one paces stood three elm trees.

"Which one?" exclaimed James.

"Father's pace and mine will be slightly different, so I'm not sure. But the clue should be by one of these three," Giles said. He started giving instructions.

"James, you, Mary and William look around that one," pointing to the nearest.

"Terrance, you check that one nearest the cemetery gate and I'll check this one."

It didn't take long.

"I've found it," shouted Terrance. He emerged from behind the tree with a tin just like the one at the pier. As they all ran to join him, William bumped into the cemetery gate and started crying.

"William!" Mary picked him up, but other than a small cut on his chin, he seemed okay. "Don't be so clumsy!"

"Open it," Giles said. But he needn't have said anything, as Terrance already had the folded paper out.

"Let us all see," said James.

"Read it aloud," said Mary. And he did.

"A broken stone points the way to pine."

"Then you must go score and nine."

"What stone?" said James.   Giles was in deep thought. *Could be one of the gravestones.* Then out loud.

"Maybe it means one of the grave stones."

"That's it," said James. "It must mean that. Come on. Let's go into the cemetery."

"Spread out and look for a grave marker with a crack or chip, or something broken on it," said Giles.

A few moments passed and then James found it. "Look," he said. "This marker for father's great grandfather has a big crack in it."

The square marker was quite large and had a small cross on top. An inch wide crack ran from the base of the cross to the center of the stone.

"Now what," said Mary. "What's the rest of the clue mean?"

Mother and Father watched through the porch window as their children gathered around the grave stone.

"Look's like they're getting it figured out," said Margaret.

"Yes," said Giles. "I hope they like their gifts this year."

"They will, dear."

"There's got to be some distance meaning here," James said, studying the paper intently. "And pine probably refers to a tree again."

Giles turned to his brother. "Remember father telling us about measurements and quantities last month?"

James hesitated and then Terrance chimed in.

"I do, and I think I see where you're going. A *score,* remember, it's the term for twenty of something."

"Yes," James agreed. "I do remember, and that must be it. The distance must be twenty plus nine. Don't you see, the riddle says *score plus nine*. Twenty nine!"

"I'm guessing twenty-nine paces from grandfather's stone marker and I'll wager in the direction of the cross points," said Giles.

"Look," yelled Mary, "there's several pine trees over there."

"No," said James, "that's the wrong direction. Follow the arm of the cross."

Mary muttered that she was only seven, took William's hand and started walking toward a cluster of three pine trees. Giles realizing that the cross arm pointed in two directions, still followed his sister's lead. After twenty-three paces he'd reached the furthest tree and knew he'd gone the wrong way. With everyone following him, he returned to the marker and paced the opposite direction. At twenty-eight paces he reached the nearest pine tree.

"James, hand me that stick." Giles dug around the front of the tree at first. Then he noticed that the dirt just behind the trunk was loose.

"It's here, I'm sure."

And it was. Just a few inches below the surface lay one of the now familiar tins. Giles opened it and read aloud.

"Now that you've almost won,"
"Look for the work of feathered ones."
"Then you must scan afar for blue."
"Go, and to win, dig down two."

"Looks like you're almost done," said the familiar voice behind them.

"Father!" They all shouted and ran to him.

"Just checking on you. Your mother and I were just curious to see how you were doing."

Mary tugged at her father's coat. "Is this the last clue, Papa?" She still resisted the more formal name, "father," that the older boys used.

"You'll see. Good luck." With that he headed back toward the house.

Giles Jr. and James acknowledged their father, but continued to peruse the riddle.

Terrance turned to his sister. "This has to be the last clue, or it wouldn't say we've *almost won, Mary.*"

She stuck her tongue out again. Terrance returned her in kind, plus he put his thumbs at his temples and wiggled his fingers.

"Come on you two, help us with this puzzle," said Giles.

"The *feathered ones.* Do you think that refers to birds?" said James.

Giles nodded. "Terrance, come here, you're going to climb this tree."

Giles gave him a boost to the first limb and, at the same time, told him to look for a bird's nest. When he'd climbed about ten feet, he found one. "Here it is, I've found it."

"If you can see in all directions, look for something blue. Maybe a flag," said Giles, now sure he had the solution.

"Anything?" James called.

Terrance got a firm foothold and yes, he could see for what seemed like miles. He could see their farmhouse, their boat, the pier on the lake and the flagpole. Then –

"I see it. There's some kind of blue flag or cloth hanging from the old flag pole near the mausoleum."

Below, Giles turned to the others. "That's got to be it. Come on Terrance. Get down and let's go, and James, grab a shovel from the shed."

The ground near the base of the pole had been disturbed recently and using the shovel James got, Giles quickly dug down two feet and hit something that gave off a ping sound. There was a tin, similar to the others, but much larger. Giles lifted it out and removed the cover. Inside were five small packages. Each package had one of the children's names on it. Giles passed them out.

"Wow," said James, examining the new pocketknife.

Giles was likewise pleased with his pocket watch, Terrance with his two soldiers, and Mary with the little doll. William jumped for joy over his small stuffed bear. Then there were five identical, small bags, each with a drawstring.

Chapter Three

1871

"Your order sir."

Giles Duncombe hadn't realized the waiter returned with his drink.

"Oh, yes," he said. "The steak and kidney pie will be just fine, Alfred."

Had it really been twenty years, he thought. He remembered how they all came running into the house with their gifts and bags of candy. The last time he'd seen his eldest son, he was still carrying that pocket watch.

The train to Edinburgh, with a stop in York, left Charing Cross Station at half-past, so Giles had to be at the bank by ten. Mr. Brambly had the draft ready.

"Thank you for your promptness and efficiency," Giles said. He pocketed the bank draft and left without further word.

Next stop the office of his friend Hans Voorwalt, he thought as his cab pulled away from the bank.

George had expected to go directly to the station, but Sr. gave him an address on Kensington Street. The sign over the door read, Voorwalt, Ltd.

"I'll be a few minutes, George," said Giles. With that he disappeared into the building.

True to his word, Giles reappeared shortly and told George to head for the station in a hurry or they would miss the train.

As they traveled the route, it felt to Giles that George hit every rut in the road. More than once Giles almost slipped off his seat. He glanced out the curtains and didn't recognize any of the surroundings.

"George, are you taking a different way?" he asked.

"Yes. To save time I'm taking Belgrave instead of Sloane, but I hadn't counted on the rough road. Sorry."

Just when he was about to admonish George, the carriage slowed down. He looked out and recognized the Post Office on Eccleston Street and knew they were just a block from the station.

One of the porters helped George with the bags while Giles bought a copy of the *Times* and found his car. Soon he saw George walking his way, followed by the porter with the bags.

He reached into his pocket purse and took out a Shilling. "George, have him put the bags in compartment three, and then give him this," handing the Shilling to George. He checked his watch. Two minutes.

"Thank you George. "I'll be arriving back on the three-fifteen in two days."

"Yes sir." He and Giles had already discussed this, but George didn't show his employer any indication that it was old news.

With that, Giles boarded the train and found compartment three, entered and closed the door. Once seated, he pulled the pouch from the leather case in his coat pocket. He opened it slowly. He knew everything was still there, but somehow he felt reassured seeing their magnificent beauty once again.

As the train slowly pulled away, Giles relaxed and thought about the last trip he'd taken to York. Esther had dearly loved to watch the countryside move by.

1870

"I love the way the fields look like a giant yellow carpet."

Esther had been staring out the car window for some time.

"Yes, the mustard crops cover most of Yorkshire this time of year," Giles responded.

She hadn't been feeling well for several days and Giles had suggested the trip to the farm. The air in London seemed to be at its worst right now. More people meant more homes and more homes meant more chimneys. Coal was cheaper than wood, but its smoke coated everything, especially the lungs of the city inhabitants.

"Are you feeling better, dear?" he asked. He reached across and took her hand.

"Somewhat," she said. Esther continued staring and then turned to Giles. She gave his hand a slight squeeze.

"Did you write your son to let him know you're coming?"

"Yes, I did. But as usual, there was no answer," he said.

"Almost two years since you've seen Giles Jr."

Esther held his gaze for a moment and then he looked away. She knew him well enough to recognize his pain and not inquire further, but uncharacteristically, she continued.

"Giles, I've always felt so bad about the rift in your family. I just know it's because we married so soon after Margaret's death."

"It's not your fault, my dear. At least James and William seem to have accepted our marriage," he said.

"I believe Catherine has too," she said.

Esther's only child from her first marriage had moved with her husband to France in 1867, but returned for her mother's marriage.

"I just got another letter from her yesterday and she sends her love."

"That's nice. Now dear, how about we go forward and have some tea? We've got about an hour to go," Giles said.

"Yes." She rose with some difficulty and taking Giles' arm, they navigated the narrow aisle to the dining car.

After the tea and a few biscuits, Esther seemed to be her old self again. She looked up from the table and smiled at Giles.

"Will Jasper be meeting us?" she asked.

"No, not tonight. We'll catch a carriage to Dean Court and stay for the night. Jasper will pick us up there in the morning."

"Could we attend the five o'clock Evensong at the Minster?" she asked. It was their favorite church service.

Giles had checked ahead and learned that a boys choir from Manchester was singing that evening. The Minster was just a short walk from their hotel.

"Yes, dear, we will. We should be able to have a short nap and be there in time."

She smiled again. "Thank you dear."

They returned to their compartment and in what seemed like just a few minutes, the train was on the outskirts of York.

The Dean Court was on Stonegate near the Minster and just a block from the Ouse River. They hadn't stayed at the Dean for some time, but had fond memories of their first stay. He and Esther had joked about it walking back from vespers. The lift for the hotel was very small. Barely enough room for two people, let alone two with luggage. The door of the lift car was a sliding glass panel, making the inside visible as the lift traveled from floor to floor. They had entered the lift and pushed the button for the third floor. Then, relieved to finally be alone, they embraced and kissed. Two elderly ladies, waiting at the second floor, got quite a show as they passed. Giles and Esther smiled at them.

"I still laugh about that time we were in the lift," she said as Giles joined her for breakfast on the balcony of their room.

"Yes, that was something. Remember how we hoped we wouldn't see them again and they ended up sitting next to us at dinner the next night?"

She nodded. "Yes, I do." Then she rose and gave her husband a kiss.

"What a beautiful morning. Look, you can see well beyond the spires on the Minster."

"I'm glad you're feeling so well this morning, my dear," he said.

Esther caught a cold the previous month and it was hanging on much too long. Giles had several times suggested a visit to the family doctor, Goeffrey Winslow, but Esther declined. She assured Giles that she was getting better. But she was not. Yesterday when they boarded the train he was sure he noticed her grimacing as she climbed the three steps into their car.

"What time will Jasper be here?" she said. Then continuing

without an answer, "I'd like to visit that little clock shop on Cronkle Street if we have time." Clocks were her passion.

"Yes, we will have time. He should be here around ten and I'm sure he won't leave without us," he chuckled. "Oliver should be with him to help." He smiled broadly. "And I'm sure we can find room at the farm for one more clock."

When they returned just before ten, Jasper was already there and loading their bags into the carriage.

"Good morning Sir. Mrs. Duncombe."

"Jasper." Giles was somewhat shocked at how old the caretaker looked. Then he remembered that he was a year older than Jasper, and like him, a grandfather.

"I'd have thought that young Oliver would have come with you," said Giles.

"No, my grandson had other things to do today."

Jasper's son John and daughter-in-law lived just west of York, and their children, Oliver and Dorothy, would often stay with their grandparents at the Duncombe farm.

"Yes, I see. Young people these days seem to have much to occupy their time." He handed Jasper the package he was carrying.

"Here's something else to pack, and carefully too." The bracket clock had cost a pretty penny, but James Perrott's craftsmanship was much esteemed and Esther was elated.

The hotel staff helped Jasper finish loading and they were on their way to the farm. Giles silently hoped the rest would do Esther some good. He definitely would insist she see the doctor when they returned to London.

The news was not good.

Giles was sitting in the doctor's office when Winslow returned from the examining room.

"Esther is getting dressed, Giles. She'll be here in a minute. I'll need a day to look over my notes, but it doesn't look promising."

"It isn't fair," said Giles. "Is it her lungs? Pneumonia?"

"Yes, I'm afraid that's it. I'm going to give her some strong medicine to try to control the coughing and then suggest you contact me tomorrow afternoon."

"If it's as bad as you think, how long does she have?"

"Hard to say for sure with pneumonia, but I'd venture two, maybe three months. Her lungs have been severely weakened."

They stopped their conversation when Esther entered the office, taking the chair next to Giles. She looked at both of them.

"That bad, huh?"

"Yes, I'm afraid it is. I'll know for sure tomorrow. I'm sorry, Esther."

While Dr. Winslow continued talking to Esther, Giles was thinking to himself. *Margaret dead only two years and now Esther soon to go too.* He was lost in thought as Winslow addressed him.

"Giles, Giles. I'll leave you two alone for a few minutes and then I'll see you tomorrow. I'll have my nurse get you some strong cough medicine, so pick it up on your way out."

He closed the door and they were alone.

"Oh, Giles, why, why?"

"I know my dear, but we won't know for sure that it's as bad as it sounds till tomorrow. Let's keep up our spirits."

But, deep down, they both knew.

"All right dear," she said. "Let's get the medicine and go home."

As they left the doctor's office, Giles thought, *Two, three months, maybe longer. They'd fight this together.*

But, it was not to be.

A month later Esther was gone.

Catherine had been with them those last few days and Terrance's wife Evelyn had come from Bath. Giles didn't know what he would have done without the help of those two women and his cook, Jenny Smythe.

The funeral service was beautiful. The absence of Giles Jr. and Mary, however, weighed heavily on Giles. Even though his marriage to Esther had enraged Giles Jr. and alienated Mary, they should have at least come to console him.

Giles was a different man after the funeral. He completely turned over the business to James and became a recluse. Whether his isolation and lack of attention to his person contributed to his declining health, Doctor Winslow was never sure, but it was a harbinger for the future. His decline accelerated as the day of reading Esther's will approached.

Malcolm had contacted Giles two days after the funeral service and suggested the following Monday so as to accommodate Catherine and her husband, Andre. They were staying with Andre's sister in Dover.

The will was simple, as Giles had recalled. An amount of 120 pounds was left to Catherine as well as most of her jewelry and several of her personal belongings. To Giles she left the two jeweled brooches he gave her on their wedding day and first anniversary. No mention was made of her wedding ring, however; it had been removed and given to Giles. Finally, there was a letter for Giles to be read by him alone.

"Here, Giles, this is for you." The letter was dated just three days before her death.

"I'll read it later," he said. But he forgot.

Catherine, her husband Andre Fontaine, William and Terrance all returned home. James lingered for the rest of the day. Giles spoke to him only once and that was to ask him to attend the printing company owner's meeting, two days hence, in his absence.

And that was that. He sat for days. Both George and Jenny tried to get him to come downstairs and eat, to no avail. He searched his mind for the logic of it all and to try and find someone to blame for his woes. Then he remembered the letter. His jacket lay on the bed and the letter was where he'd put it, in the inside pocket. Tearing open the seal, he began to read.

25 April 1871

"My dearest husband,"

"Our life together has been short but wonderfully fulfilling. When Monty was killed at Sevastopol, I was left to raise Catherine on my own. I never thought I'd fall in love and marry again."

Giles paused as he felt tears welling up. He sat down at his desk and continued reading.

"I know you grieved deeply for Margaret and at first I thought your attentions to me were misplaced. I soon realized you truly loved me. The reaction of your children was to be expected. Our marrying so soon after their mother's death was hard for them to accept. You and I hoped they would mellow and accept our union."

"For William it came slowly and I think he is still having acceptance problems and may, in fact, feel quite disassociated from the family in general. James and Terrance seem the most accepting. Giles Jr. and Mary have never accepted me and for that I am deeply sorry. I sensed, early on, however, that there was already dissension between Giles and James over your business interests. Also, Mary and Terrance seem to have some on-going animosity."

"You and your children were so close. Deep down, I know the present problems are not all my fault, but still, I have always felt a burden of guilt. It's as if my bursting in on the scene just intensified the situation."

"Giles Dear, you must do something to bring your family back together before it's too late. Maybe my death will somehow make that easier. Mourn for me, but focus on this task. Do it for me. Do it for yourself. Life is indeed too short."

"Your loving wife"

She had signed the letter in her usual strong hand, belying her weak condition.

Giles wept. He reread the letter several times.

"Yes!" he shouted, "I will do it."
I'll do it for you, Esther, and for me.

The sudden jerk of the train brought Giles back to the reality of June, 1871. *This must be Thornton,* he thought. Thornton was the last stop before York. It would be a twenty-minute stop, so Giles went forward for some tea.

"Thank you," he said to the waiter. He looked out the dining car window and thought about the past several months and the events that chartered this trip, perhaps his final one to York.

It was on another train ride that he conceived the plan to unite his family. It was on a trip to Warwickshire and the city of Leamington.

Chapter Four

Giles developed his plan on a train ride to Leamington. He'd been invited by his friend Clarence Hawthrone to spend the weekend. Clarence was the headmaster at Leamington College and he usually invited Giles and his wife to spend some time when the heat of summer in London became unbearable. They'd been classmates at Eldon.

Clarence's residence was on Kenilworth Road, just east of Binswood Avenue. The roads and avenues were lined on both sides by luxurious trees, which presented a newcomer with the feeling of being in the middle of a forest. Clarence's brother, Nathaniel, once called the city, "Leafy Leamington."

Giles and Margaret met Clarence's American brother during his sojourn in Leamington in 1855. This next year, Clarence would become the Principal of Harrow, but planned to maintain the family house in Leamington. Giles had only visited twice in the past several years: once in '64 for the memorial service for Nathaniel and then last year with Esther.

It was while he was thinking about Nathaniel's service that he had his epiphany.

He would organize a treasure hunt like in the old days. He sketched out the scenario. First step would be to enlist the help of James. It would be great fun and he hoped that now with Esther's death, Mary, at least, would participate. It would be difficult to forgive her and Giles for not attending the funeral, but he must. Secondly, he would go to York and confront Giles. He should have done it two years ago. It was time to settle their differences over the selection of James to manage the firm and his marriage to Esther. Easing the rift between Mary and Terrance over Terrance's affair might be a greater challenge, but he felt up to the task.

On the day he was to leave for York, Giles felt a sharp pain on his left side as he got out of bed. It disappeared while he was shaving, then reappeared while he dressed. *Probably just a gas pain*, he thought. But he also felt light-headed. Distressed, but undeterred, he ate a light breakfast, read the morning *London Times* and called for George to get the cab. The train for York left Victoria station at ten, so he had ample time. Halfway through the financial section, the pain gripped him again. This time it was centered in his chest. He rose from his chair and pulled the cord to summon Jenny. As he did, there was another sharp pain.

"Damn!" He held onto his chair and called Jenny, but she was already coming through the doors from the pantry.

"Jenny, get George, will you please."

She saw senior's ashen face and heard the urgency in his voice and quickly left to get George in from the carriage house.

He arrived to find Giles doubled over in his chair.

"George, it appears we will not be going to Victoria Station today."

George and Jenny helped him into the cab and George lost no time in getting Giles to Middlesex Hospital. Before they left the house, George also sent a messenger for Doctor Winslow.

Although he still felt light-headed, Giles' pains had not reoccurred and he convinced himself he was feeling much better by the time the doctor arrived. Winslow found him in a private examination room just off the main entrance hallway.

"Sorry I didn't get here any faster, Giles."

"No, that's fine. I'm sorry to bother you. I think it was just gas and the pain seems to have gone now," Giles said.

"Maybe, but let's take a good look anyway."

An hour later, Winslow had performed every test he knew. He poked and prodded every part of Giles' body, or at least to Giles, it seemed so.

"Giles, I'll be back in a minute."

Winslow was an experienced physician and he was 90% sure the pains were symptomatic of a heart attack and not gas, but he needed another opinion and sought out Doctor John Bosley who he'd learned happened to be in the hospital. He found him in the next ward and without a lot of preamble, described Giles' symptoms. Bosley listened intently and then suggested he have a look at the patient too.

"Giles," he said as he reentered the room, "this is my colleague Doctor John Bosley and I've asked him to check you over too."

Giles nodded. "Fine, but I'm feeling much better."

Ignoring the pronouncement, Bosley took Giles' hand and checked his pulse. Then he listened to his breathing and checked his eyes. For another twenty minutes he went over all the tests previously done by Winslow, plus he had Giles jump up and down on first his left leg, and then his right.

"Any pain?"

"No," said Giles, almost too emphatically. He was more out of breath than he wanted to admit and felt the now familiar tightness in the chest.

Bosley rechecked Giles' pulse and listened to his heart. Then he turned to Winslow and nodded. Winslow spoke first.

"Giles, we're fairly certain you've had a heart attack, followed by a series of small strokes. I think you know that."

Giles started to speak, but Winslow continued.

"I want you to stay here tonight and have a good rest," he said. "I'll check on you in the morning and we'll repeat some of the tests, just to make sure."

Again Giles started to speak, but Winslow continued on.

"No, no arguments. For your own good, you need to stay the night just to make sure you're out of danger. I'll explain to your man George and tell him to return in the morning."

The dining car jerked once, then again, and Giles was brought back to the reality of the present once again. He couldn't believe that it was just a short time ago that he'd left Middlesex Hospital. That had been a black day.

He rose and returned to his car. The walk and having to brace against the sideward movement took its toll. He was out of breath when he finally sat down in his compartment. He felt some pain in his chest. Quickly he drank from the small vial Doctor Winslow had given him.

So now, here he was. It was the last leg of the day's agenda. One day at the farm should do it and then back to London. He would meet with Malcolm one more time. He knew his barrister was at wit's end, but so be it. His last thought as he drifted off to sleep was that he was sorry he might not be part of the game. The hunt. The reunion.

Malcolm Jones reread the letter from Giles Duncombe given to him at their last meeting. He removed the five letters from the larger envelope. Each letter was clearly written in Giles' hand and sealed with wax. Six One-Penny stamps were affixed to each, five more than required for local postage, which he'd thought odd. As he started to reread the telegram he had composed, Malcolm sensed his clerk's presence and looked up.

"Yes, Thomas?"

"Mr. James Duncombe is here, sir."

"Yes, show him in Thomas."

Malcolm could see the tension in James' face and his normally bright eyes were dull. He rose as James entered. "James, how are you this morning?" Then realizing how banal that sounded under the circumstances, he started to apologize, but James responded first.

"I guess as fine as one could be after making funeral arrangements for one's father."

"I am sorry, James. One never really knows what to say at times like this. Please, take a chair."

James' large, tall frame barely fit the small office chair. Once seated, he removed his snuffbox from his vest pocket and inhaled a pinch. Malcolm detested the habit, which now seemed to be in vogue with the younger set. He much preferred his pipe. He handed James the draft of the telegraph message that would be sent to his siblings, informing them of their father's death the previous day.

James seemed to take forever, but finally looked up.

"This looks fine." Then he noticed the sheaf of papers and the envelopes on Malcolm's desk. He recognized his father's handwriting.

"What are these?" he said rising and pointing to the papers.

"Part of your father's instructions, but I'm sorry his wishes are not to be discussed at this time."

James' expression mirrored his displeasure at the response.

"I don't understand -------."

Malcolm interrupted him mid-sentence.

"These letters are to be posted to you and the others today, and, as I interpret his instructions, you will then understand the terms of his will. He also implied to me that after reading the letter, you, your brothers and sister would be required to be present for further revelations."

"What do you mean, 'further revelations'?"

"James, I just don't know. Wait for the letter and then we'll all know. Now, please, let's go over these details for the service."

Resigned, and having little choice, James cooperated, but left the office with a feeling that Malcolm knew more than he had told him.

Ruth Duncombe could tell from the look on her husband's face that something terrible had happened. Both children were home, so that wasn't it. *Giles was never home this early,* she thought.

"What is it dear? Something happen at school?"

"No, quite the contrary. It's father. He's dead."

"Good lord," Ruth said. "When, how?"

"The cable came just an hour ago. It was from his barrister, Malcolm Jones."

Giles went on. "Apparently he's had some heart problems for some time and had a major stroke yesterday."

"You should have answered that letter from him last week, Giles," she said. Then wished she hadn't said it.

She and Giles sat down and she took his hand in hers. "I'm sorry, I shouldn't have said that."

"No, you're right. The cable says the funeral is to be Sunday. That's in five days."

Just then the children, Sarah and Michael ran into the room.

"Father, Father, you're home."

"Yes, and I'm afraid I have some bad news about your grandfather."

The letter arrived the next day.

The telegraph lines had only extended to Bath for a few years and both businesses and individuals relied on a messenger service from the lone telegraph office on Hensley Street. Terrance and Evelyn were just finishing their tea when there was a knock on the door. Stephen stopped playing with his toy soldiers and rushed to answer.

"Stephen, wait. Let Father get the door," Evelyn said.

In a moment Terrance reentered the sitting room. His face was ashen. His gray eyes were filled with tears.

"What is it Terry?"

"It's father. He had a stroke. He's dead."

The letter to Terrance was in the next day's mail when Evelyn went to the post office.

Tyler Kirkland wished his wife had reconciled with her father and brothers, especially Terrance. She still felt strong indignation over Terrance's affair and Tyler knew how she had resented her father's marriage to Esther. Nevertheless, he had tried to get Mary to attend Esther's funeral and almost went by himself to at least represent the family. He knew that she continued to correspond with her brother Giles in York, and it seemed she was still close to William, but they had not seen him in some time.

Tyler looked up from his desk at Brandon Milling as Constance ushered in the messenger.

He read the telegram slowly, then reached for his coat and walked to his secretary's desk.

"Constance, I'm going to have to go home now," he said.

She nodded. "Will you be returning today?"

"I doubt it. It's my father-in-law. He had a stroke and died."

"Oh, I'm terribly sorry sir. Tell your wife, Mary, that I'll keep her in my prayers."

"Thank you, Constance," he said while donning his coat.

Two days later another of the letters posted by Malcolm arrived for Mary.

William Duncombe's housekeeper, Mrs. Prentise, took the cable from the messenger. It was marked urgent, but Mr. Duncombe's friend, Mr. Keith told her that her employer wouldn't return for two more days. She placed the envelope on the receiving table and continued her house cleaning chores.

Ethel Prentise didn't much like Mr. Keith, especially the way he answered her when she asked about the steamer trunk that morning. Later, when he left, she reread the shipping tags. "B. Duncan, o/b Blackadder, Pier 2, South Hampton."

She thought to ask again, anyway, if Keith returned before she was finished. But being told that it was none of her business, grated on her. *What a pompous man Mr. Keith is*, she thought. When she finished cleaning the study and Mr. Keith had not returned, she got her coat and departed. Tomorrow was her day off, but when she came back, she intended to ask about the trunk.

Much later, when Edward Keith returned to the house, he noted the telegram but momentarily left it untouched.

Before William left, he had arranged for Edward to pick up his accumulated mail at the Post Office. Keith hastily removed the letters from his jacket, retrieved the telegram and placed them all in one of the steamer trunk compartments. Just in time too, as the men came for the trunk an hour later. He would have to remember to tell William tomorrow, when he saw him in South Hampton.

James was with his father in the hospital. It had been a dreadful experience. After his return from York, Giles Sr. seemed improved. Then two days later, he suffered a massive stroke. Doctor Winslow advised James to contact the other family members immediately. A day passed and there was no improvement, but James still hesitated. He had talked his father into writing Giles Jr. the previous week, but the letter was never answered.

Then, as James sat by the bed trying to decide what to do, he heard a sudden intake of breath and his father was gone.

Now, sitting in his study, he thought about all that had happened and hoped that his brothers and sister would come to their father's funeral service. Perhaps a reading of the will the day following would provide enough incentive. And what about the letters he'd seen?

That same day the postman delivered a letter. He recognized his father's handwriting on the envelope and immediately knew this was one of the letters he'd seen in Malcolm's office. What was going on?

That question wasn't answered completely after he read the letter, but he was now sure that everyone would be at the service. Even in death, his father was still the game player. He picked up the letter again, and slowly reread it, still amazed at what was obviously part of his father's plan to bring the family together.

"Children"

"You will likely be attending my funeral soon if you are reading this letter. Malcolm knows the terms of the will, which are quite simple. But beyond that, I have left the bulk of my wealth to you. To receive it, however, will require you to solve several riddles and work together. I love you all."

To my beloved children I dedicate this game.
Solve the riddles, open a name, a fortune you'll claim.
Save the envelopes you received from me.
All five are necessary of that you'll see.
Examine the postage. Consider some steam.
Reverse the image to achieve your dream.
The clues are there in perfect order, that's right,
You'll find the treasure when you all unite.

When he was in London, he often met her at The Kenilworth on Drury Lane. This time, however, she again opted for the Vanderbilt, which was in a quieter section of Knightsbridge, where they stayed the last several times. The most recent was four months ago when he broke off the relationship. She twice telegraphed him at his publishing firm, but he had not answered. On the train ride from Bath he told Evelyn that after he dropped them off at his father's home, he must go to his London office.

Why did I send her that telegram, he thought as the carriage made the turn off Gloucester onto Cromwell and stopped in front of the hotel. She had telegraphed back that she would meet him and register under the name she'd previously used, Mrs. Helen Lloyd. *Damn,* he thought again, *I told Mary this affair was over and here I am again.*

They met three years ago at a birthday party for his nephew Michael at the Duncombe home. James brought her to the party and once Terrance saw her, he couldn't take his eyes off her, and hoped it wasn't too obvious. During one brief exchange, he learned she was a student at the secretarial school in Clyde Park and worked nights as a seamstress.

The affair began slowly but soon he was going to London more often than actually required in his business and she had traveled to Bath twice when Evelyn and Stephen visited her parents in Burton On Trent. It was on one of their nights in London that Tyler Kirkland saw them together. Tyler had been dining with some suppliers at Finley's, a popular restaurant next to the Kenilworth, and was leaving just as they were entering the hotel. Terrance introduced Anne as a co-worker, Helen, from the office, but it was obvious from Tyler's expression that he remembered her from the party.

Terrance felt he could almost guarantee that Tyler would tell Mary. He was as hen pecked as a man could be and Terrance knew from past experience that Tyler told Mary everything. Sure enough, he got a letter from her two days later at his office. At least she hadn't written him at home where Evelyn would ask about the letter. He wrote back the following week and as it was likely obvious, he admitted the dalliance, told her it was his first and that he would end it that very week. As far as he knew she believed him and never said anything to Evelyn or any of the other members of the family. That was almost three years ago.

"Good evening Mr. Lloyd, your wife has already picked up the key and said she would wait for you in the lounge." Jensen, the night manager, had been at the Vanderbilt for some time and was always solicitous when Terrance and Anne stayed there. They used the names Helen and Donald Lloyd when registering.

He walked to the dimly lit room and spotted her right away. Anne Spencer was a free spirit and had always challenged the social customs of the day. Being the only unaccompanied female in the lounge didn't bother her a bit. She was having a glass of wine and to further irritate the men present, was smoking a cigarette.

"I thought you said it was over, Terry," she said teasingly, blowing a ring of smoke his way.

"I know, but I just had to see you."

"Terry, it's been four months. Life's gone on. Besides, you know I can't leave Henry alone and I had one hell of a time finding someone to watch him."

He nodded and sat down. *God*, he thought, *when I'm near her I'm just like a moth drawn to flame.* Ann wasn't a traditional beauty, but her long blond hair, translucent blue eyes and full red lips were mesmerizing. Just her presence in the room caused every nerve in his body to tingle. The waiter came to their table and he ordered a pink gin and accepted one of her cigarettes.

"I know this is awkward, but something's happened. Father's dead. That's why I'm in London."

"Dead. When?" She snuffed out her cigarette.

"Three days ago. The will is to be read tomorrow," he said. He finished his pink gin and ordered another, Anne, too. For awhile they sat in silence. Anne reached over and took his hand. She thought to herself. *All that money and not one shilling for Henry or me. Doesn't seem fair.* Terrance rose.

"Listen, I'd feel a lot better talking about it in the privacy of the room," he said.

"You sure that's all it will be, Terry, just conversation?"

He looked hurt and she wished she hadn't been cynical. Anne's life since their breakup had been rough. Terrance regularly sent her money, but that, plus her seamstress wages barely covered their expenses. The small flat on Baker Street took most of her money, and lately, Henry seemed to be growing out of his clothes. He was a big boy for two years.

They made their way down the familiar hallway to the room they had shared for so many nights.

"Oh look, just the same," she said as they entered.

Terrance didn't answer, but took off his jacket and filled one of the glasses on the bureau with water. He could feel her eyes on his back. *This is going to be tough*, he thought. She still caused that feeling of desire that he experienced since the first time they met. The thin blouse she was wearing did nothing to quell the rising sensation he was feeling.

"Anne, I have no idea what's in father's will, but as he knew nothing about our relationship or Henry, there's no reason to expect anything." She started to talk, but he continued.

"I will try to increase your monthly payment if I can. I still have to be careful. I think Mary may still be suspicious. Besides, I'm not really sure there will be much of an inheritance. You see, father left a rather cryptic letter with a riddle that has to be solved."

"A riddle? You have to solve a riddle to get any money?"

"It appears so," he said. "Listen, I've got to use the loo, so just give me a minute. Here, you might as well see for yourself." He reached for his jacket pocket and handed her the envelope. She read the letter with amusement. Terry had told her about his father's propensity for games and riddles. After reading the letter a second time, she examined the envelope. *Nothing unusual*, she thought.

She heard the water running and figured he was washing up. She remembered that this had always been his routine just before they had sex. Then it would be her turn and when she came out he was most usually already in bed, naked and eager. *Not tonight*, she thought. She looked at the letter again. *Damn, Henry should have part of this. It isn't fair!*

Terrance emerged fully clothed and sat on the edge of the bed.

"So, what do you think, Anne? Can you make any sense out of it?"

"I think it's all crazy." She began to realize that part of his night's motive was to see if she could help him solve the riddle. *What effrontery! She had been right to be cynical.*

She got up from the chair and sat next to him. "No, I don't think I can help and I think it's time for me to go."

"Wait, Anne, why don't you at least stay a while longer?"

"No, you and I both know that we'd end up like always."

She gave him a quick kiss on the cheek, rose and without a backward glance, left the room and headed to her station.

There's got to be a way for Henry and I to get our share.

Chapter Five

The *S S Blackadder* was a fullrigged iron clipper ship built the previous year and making its maiden voyage to America. William had booked passage more than a month ago. He had just finished the morning meal and was strolling around the first class passenger's deck. This was his first time at sea and the steward had suggested he acclimate himself as much as possible while they were still in calm waters. William couldn't believe how large the ship was. The forecastle was thirty-four feet long and the poop deck thirty feet. One of the Mates told him that the Blackadder was named after a river in Berwickshire and had already made voyages to Shanghai and the Cape. Apparently, the voyage to the Cape was not completed due to some problem with one of the masts, but Edward had assured him that the ship was now remasted and ready for duty.

Edward Keith had done most of the arranging for him through a contact at the owners, John Willis & Son of London. Using a false name had proved to be a bit tricky, but eventually all his papers were in order and his steamer trunk arrived on schedule.

William took another turn around and returned to his cabin. *It was cold for the 12th of October*, he thought.

The previous afternoon and evening's activities were still fuzzy in his memory. Everything happened so fast, that he hadn't yet found time to unpack the rest of his trunk. Most of what he needed for the voyage lay piled on the dressing table and he figured the rest could wait till they reached New York. Last evening he had worn his one set of good clothes to dinner, as Edward had arranged for him to sit at the captain's table. Captain John Robinson was a gracious host and obviously relished the opportunity to inform his table guests about the *Blackadder,* especially about the maiden voyage to Shanghai.

There was a knock at the door.

"Yes, what is it?"

"Mr. Duncan, we've spotted some whales off the port side and the captain thought the passengers would like to see them."

He and Lenora had agreed to meet at two and it was now quarter of. *He would have a few minutes*, he thought.

"Yes, thank you, I'd like to do that."

He reached for his jacket and then checked his image in the mirror. Last night had been a test. Without the beard and mustache he looked quite different, but he was fearful that someone might recognize him. He did not see anyone he knew. Still, he had to continue to be careful. He had almost goofed at dinner when the chief steward had called his name for seating. He hoped Lenora would remember to call him Ben instead of William. He had opted for Bill as a first name, but Edward said it was too close to William.

Leaving his cabin, he noticed the crowd at the rail and joined them to watch the pod of whales off to port. After a few minutes, he left and made his way to the stairs that led down to the second class deck and Lenora's cabin. He hadn't gotten used to calling a ship's stairway a ladder.

It was only a half-hour before the service and William still hadn't arrived. Most of the family were gathered at the rectory next door. James and Giles seemed to have resigned themselves to being civil, but Terrance stood off by himself, not quite sure he wanted to talk to anyone, especially Mary, who was now walking toward him.

"Terrance, you are the only one of us that has recently seen William. Do you have any idea if he's coming or not?"

"I'm sure he'll be here. He and father were still close," he said. He noticed with some satisfaction Mary's grimace at his inference.

"Yes, Terry." James joined them. "Can you see any reason why William wouldn't be here?"

"As I just said to Mary, no, but if he doesn't get here, I'm sure there's a good explanation."

Just then the rector entered and told them it was time to proceed to the church and take their places. The children, Sarah and Michael Duncombe, Stephen Duncombe and Olivia Kirkland, under Ruth's watchful eye, had already left. Mary's husband, Tyler, and Terrance's wife, Evelyn, waited just outside the parsonage door.

"Well, with or without William, here we go," said James.

He had asked Giles if, as the eldest, he wanted to deliver the eulogy, but he declined, so the task fell to James. He didn't mind and in fact felt honored. The eulogy had gone well as had the rest of the service and the brief graveside ceremony. At the conclusion, the rector announced that all were invited to gather for tea and sandwiches at the Duncombe residence. At the gathering, Malcolm Jones reminded each of the siblings of the will reading at ten the next morning, and to bring their letters.

Mary and Tyler and their daughter Olivia were staying with James at his flat in London. After Olivia was put to bed, the three adults gathered in James' study.

"Some brandy?"

"Yes, thank you," they both answered.

"Do you mind if I smoke James?" asked Tyler.

"No, of course not, and I'll join you." He reached for the humidor, opened it and offered Tyler a cigar.

"No thanks, I'll have my pipe, but go ahead."

"Mary?" He smiled broadly.

"James, you know I can't stand those things, but at least they are not as filthy as that tobacco you sniff up your nose!"

"Ah, touché," he said. He closed the humidor and proceeded to clip the ends of the cigar. Then, in a more serious tone he looked up at Mary and spoke.

"All right, what do you make of father's letter? I assume we all got the same one."

"I assume so, let me see yours," she said.

James rose and went to his desk, opened the top drawer and removed the now familiar letter.

"Here," he said handing it to her.

Mary took one look and knew it was the same as her own and James sensed from her reaction, that it was too.

"Yes, the same," she said and then continued.

"Have you tried to figure out what it means?"

"No, but I think old Malcolm knows more than he's letting on. Do you want to spend some time now with this riddle or should we wait for Giles and Terrance?"

"I say we try to figure it out now," Mary said. "Tyler, you can help."

"All right, dear. James, let's have another brandy. Maybe that will get us in the mood for riddles and I'll try one of those cigars now," Tyler said.

At the Duncombe home, Giles and Terrance and their families said a few pleasantries to each other and then went to their separate rooms. Jenny took the children to the third floor and put them to bed. Jenny and George had offered them all some food, but they declined, although Stephen had whined a bit, claiming he was still hungry.

Giles sat in the chair by the window while Ruth prepared for bed. He was reading the letter for the third time. *"Save the envelopes."* He looked at the envelope. It was common enough. His address in York was written in his father's familiar hand. *Wait a minute*, he thought. *Why the extra postage? It was still only a pence to York from London.* He looked at the riddle again. *"All five are necessary."* And, *"Examine the postage."*

In another bedroom down the hall, Terrance and Evelyn were looking over the letter and had come to the conclusion that the use of five extra penny post stamps might be related to the "five" mentioned in the riddle. The riddle had clearly stated they were to examine the postage.

Terrance had tried to get Stephen interested in one of the current hobbies in London, "Plating Victoria," so he was somewhat familiar with the postage labels. The goal was to reconstruct the full plate of 240 labels. On the plate, each label differed from the other by the letters in the four corners. Each label was individually engraved and contained the plate number in its margin. The top right label corners were engraved AA, the next in the row AB, AC and so forth. The next row started with position BA, then BB and continuing on till the last position, BL. A full sheet of labels from the plate was twelve across and twenty down, for a total of 240.

Terrance had noted that his six penny postage labels, or stamps, as some were calling them, were positions DA, DB, DC, DD, DE and DF. Evelyn was reading the letter and riddle again.

"Terry, it says here to *'consider some steam,'* how odd."

The next morning Malcolm Jones arrived at half past nine, shortly followed by Mary, Tyler and James. Terrance had given George a cable to send to William earlier, but still hoped he would show up for the reading of the will. It had also occurred to him that the riddle had been clear about, *"all five are necessary."* Terrance assumed that meant all five children, not a reference to the five extra postage labels. But that could be too.

At a few minutes before ten they all gathered in the living room. James noted that both Jenny and George were present.

"Thank you all for being so prompt," Malcolm said.

"I have asked George and Jenny to be present, for as you will hear, they are mentioned in your father's will. Secondly, let me say that I am not privy to the contents of the letters you received. They were sealed when I got them from Giles. I know they are intended to facilitate a reconciliation between you and result in you each receiving an equal share of your father's wealth. That William is not here may or may not affect your effort. I just don't know. Let us proceed to the reading of the will."

"To my faithful servants and I must say, friends, Jenny and George, I leave the sum of 100 pounds and the condition that they continue to be employed at the London Duncombe residence for at least the next five years, if it is their wish. Additionally, that their wages be increased by 10% during such employment. My house in London I bequeath to my son James, who is authorized to rent the property or use it himself as he sees fit. Also, I authorize James to dispose of my personal belongings and donate the proceeds to a charity of his choosing. I have instructed Malcolm Jones to sell my shares in Derkins Printing and divide the proceeds equally to each of my children and by stripes to their children. My shares in Duncombe Shipping are to be divided as follows: 30% to James, 20% to Giles, 20% to Terrance and 15% each to Mary and William. James will continue to manage the firm. The property in York I leave to my eldest son, Giles, with the provision that Jasper and Edythe continue to be employed as long as they wish, for at least the next five years. The balance of my estate, save the sum for George and Jenny, has been liquidated and is the treasure you will find if you cooperate as you used to when you were young. It is a sizeable sum. By now, Malcolm has already mailed your letters. Malcolm also has an envelope that reveals the location of the treasure. The envelope is in a safe at Malcolm's London office. He does not know the contents, only the combination of the safe. If, after two years, the treasure is not found, he will open the envelope, retrieve the treasure and donate the value to a charity of his choice. Malcolm has selected an alternate at his firm to perform these functions in the event of his incapacity or death prior to the two years elapsing. So, go for it. Work together. You must. I love you all, your father, Giles Duncombe."

Of the five children, Mary had facial features that most mirrored her father's in his later years. Even at twenty-eight she was beginning to show that sour expression most of the time, especially when she was under stress, and at the moment, she was definitely stressed.

"This is ridiculous," she cried. "How utterly stupid! What did he think he was doing? And why should James get this house?"

She turned and started to leave the room, with Tyler close behind. Then she turned back abruptly, almost knocking Tyler down. "Jenny, some tea, if you please. I'm going to the solarium."

Of the brothers, James spoke first.

"I agree with Mary, it is ridiculous, but not unlike something Father would have done. To me, we don't have much choice. Malcolm, any thoughts? But then, you haven't seen the letters we got, have you?"

Malcolm rose from behind the desk and took his pipe from his vest pocket. The others watched as he filled it and waited patiently for him to answer.

"You're correct, I have not seen the letters, but I am aware of your father's scheme and that he has secreted somewhere a sum well over 300,000 pounds. Originally, he planned to be present during your search and was almost giddy about the five of you working together to find the treasure as you had in your youth. When he knew he was close to death, he still decided to proceed, but with some changes, only known to him, as far as I am aware. I was not privy to the final concept, only that it was still his wish that you all work together and equally share in the rewards. That's all I can tell you."

James turned toward Giles. "Anything to add, brother?"

Jenny left the room to make some tea and after hearing what Malcolm had to say, George also departed to the kitchen. Giles, ignoring his brother's question, moved to the liquor cabinet and removed a bottle of Talisker.

"James, Terry, I don't know about you, but I need a drink."

They nodded and he poured out four glasses.

"Here." He handed them their glasses and then took a healthy swig of the single malt scotch.

"Now to your question, little brother. I agree we have no choice. I'm sure both you and Terry have already tried to decipher the riddle in the letter. I'm guessing Mary has, too. I don't think it's going to be that hard. But here's the rub. It's clear to me that father fully intended that all five of us participate and I'm betting that, without William, we may have a problem."

"I agree," said Terrance, speaking for the first time. He walked past James and poured himself another scotch.

"Giles? It's not every day you can drink Talisker's."

"No, thanks, I think we all need a clear head. Right Malcolm?"

They'd briefly forgotten about the barrister, who now finished his drink and began putting papers in his briefcase.

"I'd say you are right, Giles. However, I must bid you all good day. Good luck. I'll be preparing the documents required to satisfy your father's wishes and be in contact with you in a few days. I would add this much, however, I concur that locating William is of prime importance."

With that, he left the room.

"I still think he knows more than he lets on," said James.

"Well, it doesn't really matter, does it," said Giles. "Let's get Mary and see if together we can't make some sense of this confounded riddle and then figure out what happened to William."

Tyler was used to his wife's tantrums and didn't say anything, just followed her into the solarium. Slowly the color drained from her face and she began to cry.

"I'm sorry Tyler, it just got to me. Imagine, after all those years and I'm barely mentioned in his will. Then this riddle business and the chance that we won't get anything."

One of the curls in her upswept hair wrap had untwisted and fallen across her face. In an uncharacteristic gesture, Tyler reached out and pushed it from her eyes.

"Come on dear, you get ownership in the shipping company and a share of the proceeds from the sale of the printing company. That's not so bad."

That seemed to calm her and just then, Jenny arrived with the tea. That helped even more.   They drank their tea in silence and Tyler was just about to talk when James appeared.

"Sorry Mary, I didn't know what was in Father's will until just now. Come back in. We need to put our heads together and try solving the puzzle. Then there's the absence of William. Come on, Giles and Terry are waiting for us. Tyler, you too."

"All right, James, give me a minute and we'll be there," she said. Now she seemed her old self and rose to give Tyler a kiss on his cheek.

"Thank you, dear. You go ahead and join them and I'll be there shortly."

After Tyler left, she carefully rearranged her hair in its bun and using her mirror, made sure her makeup was in place. She pulled the letter from her handbag and read it once again.

Think you're so clever papa. We'll see. Six postage labels and five children. Could that be a clue? What about the reference to "steam." That didn't make sense.

She returned the letter to the envelope and left to join her brothers, who she found, had been joined by Evelyn and Ruth.

"How about the children?" Mary asked, upon entering.

"Jenny and George are watching them for now," Evelyn said.

"Any luck so far?" Mary asked no one in particular.

"We may have something, Mary. Terry has hit upon an idea involving the postage labels. Let me see your envelope," Giles said.

They all gathered around Giles and Terrance. Just like in the old days, Giles had taken over, but no one seemed to mind. He laid out the four envelopes on the desk.

"Well, Terry?" Giles asked.

"Yes, look here. Your six labels are positions AB through AF. James' are BA through BF, mine DA through DF and Mary's are plate positions EA through EF."

"Remember father's riddle referred to 'perfect order' and 'examine the postage'," Giles said. He took out his letter and held it out to them.

"Do you think the part about reversing the image means to read the letters backwards?" Mary asked.

"I'll bet that William's envelope has six labels with the letters CA through CF," Ruth said.

They all looked at her and knew she was right.

Jenny entered the room and walked over to Mary, softly said something to her and left.

"Tyler, Olivia seems to be ill and I must go help Jenny. I suggest we take a break, have something to eat and then give it a go later."

"You go ahead and tell Jenny to make us some sandwiches. We'll keep working for now and then join you when the food is ready," Giles said. *Feels good to be in charge.*

Chapter Six

The bad weather that had been predicted stayed north of their course and the *S S Blackadder* was making good time. Captain Robinson was in good spirits. When Ben inquired about meeting with him, Robinson had responded quickly and positively.

The Captain's cabin was opulent compared to even the best of the first class cabins. The spacious front room was paneled with rich, brown mahogany and each wall was adorned with what Ben assumed were souvenirs of the captain's travels. Most prominent was a huge lion's head flanked on either side by the head of a Bengal tiger. At the end opposite the cabin door was a large desk covered with a variety of nautical items including a scale model of the *Blackadder*.

Robinson did not rise when Ben entered, but motioned to one of the leather chairs in front of his desk.

"Now, Mr. Duncan, what can I do for you?"

Ben wasn't accustomed to his new first name and was having even more trouble with the name Duncan. It was almost too close to Duncombe, but he, Lenora and Edward had finally agreed.

"I wish to be married."

Ben had rehearsed a long explanation, but once he'd uttered his request, his resolve failed and he just sat still without any further comment. The captain, meanwhile, rose from his desk and walked toward Ben with a smile forming around his mouth. Ben rose to meet him.

"You do, do you? Well, that's possible, but maybe you need to tell me a little more, young man."

Ben sat back down and with some urging, began to pour out the story of his romance with Lenora, one of the reasons for their flight from Bath and their plans in the Americas.

"And where is this lucky young lady now?"

"In a cabin on second deck," Ben answered.

"Ah, the young lady I saw you with after dinner yesterday. Well, perhaps you can give me a few more details. Then, I'd like to meet your intended. That said, I see no reason why we can't perform a ceremony tomorrow. What is the lady's name?"

"Lenora Franklin."

The ceremony was performed that next morning in the captain's cabin. Lenora was not feeling well, and the ship's rolling caused by increasing winds from the south, just added to her discomfort. Captain Robinson had performed marriages at sea before and obviously was enjoying himself. He would make a note in the log that this was his first on a voyage across the Atlantic.

"There, done. Congratulations. You may kiss the bride."

"Ouch!" shouted James, pulling his hand away from the kettle.

"Hold on just another minute, James," Giles said.

Mary had rejoined the group and now she, Terrance, Evelyn and Tyler were gathered around the two brothers in the pantry. It was Giles idea to steam off the postage labels to examine the other sides. He was sure that's what the riddle directed. They were using his envelope.

"Be careful not to tear them," Mary said.

"Yes. I'm right. Look!" said Giles.

Just as Giles had guessed, the first postage label, position AA, had something printed on its reverse side. So did the second and each of the remaining four. James lay them out at random on a hand towel to dry.

Terrance and the others were all trying to get as close as they could to read the printing, which they could see were words that looked English. Each word was printed horizontally on the postage label.

"Come on! Let Giles or James read them. There's no sense in us all trying to push our way in."

"Terry's right. Step back and I'll read what's on them," said Giles.

The words on the back were *Haste, Or, Reap, You'll, Only* and *Kindled.*

"They don't make any sense," said James.

"They probably won't without the other postage labels from our envelopes," said Giles.

"Also, remember about the plating of the sheet. I think you need to arrange the words on the back in the order of the position," said Terrance. He reached across and proceeded to do so.

By evening they had steamed off all of the postage stamps and arranged them upside down in alphabetically positioned order on the living room table.

You'll only reap kindled haste Or
make each one's first delight Even
Eden's Eve used place first One
urges regarding letter each found there.

"Well, I give up," said James.

"Remember, James, we don't have William's envelope and it would give us the words on the third line," said Giles.

James nodded, walked to the nearby desk, and returned with some stationary, a nib pen and a bronze ink pot. As they watched, he meticulously copied the words from the labels.

"There," he said. "That will give us something easier to work with."

Later they still were no closer to making sense out of the words. Terrance did point out that certain words were capitalized and that might mean something. At eight they adjourned to the dining room for some cakes and an aperitif.

"We must get Olivia and leave soon," said Mary. "I propose we call it a night and meet back here tomorrow morning."

"Mary, I need to get back to the mill tomorrow. I told them I'd only be gone for a day or so," said Tyler.

Mary glared at him. "Send them a wire and let them know you'll be another day. You are the owner, you know," she said in her familiar acerbic tone.

James indicated he needed to get home too, but they agreed to work another half-hour and start fresh in the morning. Evelyn went to tell Jenny to have Stephen ready in thirty minutes. Giles and Ruth left to check on Sarah and Michael.

Mary excused herself too, saying she'd meet them in the study and James went to find George and tell him to get the carriage ready. Tyler said he'd left his tobacco in the Solarium and would be back shortly. That left Terrance alone in the dining room. He rose and opened the doors to the garden and walked out. As he did so, he was startled by movement to his left. *Had someone been watching them?* He, walked out a little further and didn't see anyone, but looking to the right he could see that the living room door was open. *Must have been my imagination*, he thought.

Finally a chance! Shall I take the postage labels? Here's the paper James was writing on. Yes, that should do. Oh, oh, someone's coming. Time to leave.

Giles was the first to get back to the living room. He stood in front of the fireplace. As James entered, Giles was adding some wood to the fire, which was now mostly embers.

"Don't put too much on, Giles, we'll be leaving soon," James said.

Ruth entered next. "Oh, there you are dear."

James was the first to notice that the paper with the words was missing.

"Giles, did you take the paper?"

Giles looked up, while at the same time, Terrance, Tyler and Mary entered the room.

"You mean the paper you wrote the riddle words on? No, of course not," Giles said incredulously. "It must be there."

Evelyn was the last to arrive. "Stephen's in bed and Jenny has Sarah and Michael just about ready, Ruth."

"Thanks, Evelyn," Ruth said. Then she turned to her husband.

"So, what's this about the paper, Giles?"

"Well, it seems that someone has taken it."

He moved next to James, who was at the moment counting the postage labels.

"They're all here, thank goodness. I'll make another copy of these and then I suggest you each retrieve your labels and letters and put them in a safe place. It appears one of us or someone else in this house has been here since we left. What anyone could gain by taking the paper, I do not know."

Seems obvious to me , dear brother, thought Mary.

While James was talking, Terrance was thinking about the open dining room door and the rustling he had heard a few minutes earlier. *I wonder?*

"In light of this, I think we should call it a night and meet here at eight tomorrow for breakfast. Also, as James has suggested, let's put these postage labels and our letters in a safe place," said Giles. He hesitated and then went on.

"I think we need to get in touch with Malcolm to get some help trying to find out about William. If it's all right with everyone, I'll have George go to Malcolm's office first thing in the morning. I'm sure he said he would be staying in London tomorrow."

"And finally, if whoever took that paper thinks they gain advantage over the rest of us, they're wrong. We need to work together on this. That was father's plan, you know."

"That's a strange comment from you, brother," said James. "You and Mary have not been particularly loving of our father these past few years."

Giles, ignoring James' snide remark, rose and motioned to Ruth. "Good night. Come along, dear. See you all at eight." Ruth followed her husband out of the living room.

George passed them as he entered the room. He walked over to Mary and James.

"The carriage is ready ma'am."

Greenwich Village – New York City – circa 1870

Chapter Seven

New York City – October 1871

Among the immigrants shown on the passenger list for the *S S Blackadder* when it reached port in New York on October 24, 1871, were Mr. & Mrs. Benjamin Duncan, of Chester, England. The signature at the bottom of the list was James Carlson, Chief Immigration Officer, Reception Headquarters, Castle Garden Station, Manhattan, New York. The ship's Purser had added a brief note that Mr. and Mrs. Duncan were married at sea on October 21, 1871.

Lenora was sure that her sister would be there to meet them, but expressed concern to Ben when their processing dragged on for three hours. At last they were finished and, as promised, there stood Martha jumping up and down with childlike excitement and waving at them as they passed through the door into the main room of the station.

It had been almost two years since Lenora and Martha had seen each other. They clung tightly together, all the while crying tears of joy. Ben gave Martha a quick hug, said he'd be right back, and left to claim their trunks.

Martha was six years older than her sister and had been in America for over a year. She mentioned in her last letter that she was seeing an Irish fellow and that it was getting serious. When she and Martha finally separated, Lenora noticed a short, light complexioned man with bright red hair, standing off to the side. His bright blue eyes seemed to sparkle and his smile broadened as he walked toward them.

"Lenora, this is Mickey."

New York in 1871 was a sprawling city of ethnically diverse districts. The tension and labor unrest growing out of the Civil War still lingered and was compounded by the increase in immigrants from Western and Eastern Europe, especially from Italy and Ireland. Michael O'Toole arrived in New York in 1870 and fortunately found work on the docks. One of the fellows he met on his voyage, Sean Larkin, told Michael of his connections at a place called Tammany Hall, and, sure enough, they both were hired by the end of their first week.

Michael and Sean shared a room in Greenwich Village, a district largely populated by Irish immigrants. Michael had decided early on that he would learn more about his new country and try to become a citizen as soon as he could. He learned from one of the fellows in their building that there was a library just two blocks away on 9th Street.

On his second visit to the Lenox Library he met Martha Franklin. Martha worked nights at the checkout desk at the library. She shared a flat on Delaware Street, within walking distance of the library. During the days, she worked in the library at Hunter College.

Martha was surprised to get the job at Hunter, but the College had just opened and there was a shortage of people with any background in library work. Martha had worked at the library in Chester for two years.

"Nice to meet you, Lenora. I see that beauty runs in the Franklin family," Mickey said with a lilt in his Irish brogue.

She smiled. "Thank you. But you may now call me Mrs. Benjamin Duncan."

Martha shrieked for joy, attracting the attention of everyone around. Ben, approaching with the trunks on a large wheeled cart, stopped to see the source of the scream and realized it came from his wife's sister Martha. He could see too that Lenora was quite embarrassed and trying to calm down her sister.

"When?" said Martha. Then, as if it just came to her. "On the boat. Yes, that's it. Oh, you silly, you could have waited until you got here."

"Well, I'm guessing you just told her about our marriage," Ben said. He could tell from the expressions that he'd been right. It was then that he noticed the short, redheaded fellow standing just behind Martha. He nodded in that direction.

"I'm Ben Duncan," he said extending his hand.

"Mickey O'Toole. Glad to meet you, and congratulations."

"This really messes up my plans for the rooms, you know, said Martha. "I had you staying with me and William, oops sorry, Ben, staying with Mickey."

"That's all right, sis, we can split up for a couple of nights while Ben and I look for a place."

Mickey could tell by the look on Ben's face that he didn't think it was such a hot idea. He couldn't blame him.

"I've got a wagon outside. Come on Ben, let's get your trunks loaded. We can stop at my place first, then go to Martha's," Mickey said. "Always happy to help the English."

London – 1871

Oren Eflow had been a private investigator for six years since retiring from Scotland Yard in '65. His small office was on Bradberry Street, just a block from Duncombe Shipping. The Duncombes had retained his services before, so it wasn't too unusual to receive a message that James Duncombe wished to see him. The note said something about locating William Duncombe, who he recalled, was the youngest son. He arrived at the yard at nine and was ushered into James' office.

"Sorry to hear about your father's passing, Sir."

"Thank you, Oren. Have a seat. Tea?" Eflow was not only tall, but quite stout, and barely fit into the small office chair.

"No thanks. So, how may I help you?"

James told Eflow most of the story. First about the letter with the riddle, then about the fact that someone had stolen the paper with the words, and finally that William was missing. He left out some of the specifics regarding the actual riddle words, but was detailed in all the rest of his information, even about how the postage labels had the clues on their back.

"But here's the thing," he said. "For now, I need you to concentrate on finding my brother. The rest Giles and I will deal with. Here, I've written down as many details as I can."

Oren reached for the paper and studied it for a moment. He noted first that the last time anyone had seen William, he was in Bath and that James had written down Terrance's address.

"Your brother, Terrance, he was the last to see William?"

"Yes." Then adding a thought, "We are not really sure he ever got the telegram or the letter."

"Where are the rest of your family now, still in London?"

"No, they have all left."

James explained that after last evening, they decided to return to their own homes: Terrance and Evelyn to Bath, Mary and Tyler to Birmingham and Giles and Ruth to York. The siblings agreed to meet at Malcolm's office in a week to sign all the papers, and in the meantime, work separately to solve the riddle.

"That should do it for now, then," said Oren. "I'll start my inquiries in Bath tomorrow."

The train ride from Victoria Station to Bath took a little over three hours with the stops in Reading and Swindon. Now the county borough of northeastern Somersetshire, Bath was fast becoming a famous vacation spot because of its renowned spa. It was the oldest of Great Britain's mineral water spas. The main part of the city was built along the Avon River. The Pulteney Publishing Company was located in the Edgar Building, near Queen Square. Oren took a cab from the station to the publishing company office on Pulteney Street, which like the publishing company, was named after Jacob Pulteney, one of the 18th century developers of the spa. His appointment was at 1 o'clock and he was early. He hadn't taken time to eat, so he was happy when Miss Wilson, the receptionist, offered him some tea and crumpets while he waited for Terrance.

After a few minutes, Terrance came into the waiting room.

"Sorry, I didn't realize you were here, detective," he said.

"No, I'm the one who is early, and by the way, it's just Mr. Eflow now, I'm in private practice."

Terrance answered Eflow's questions concerning William's whereabouts as best he could.

"And you say you haven't seen him in several weeks. Can you be more specific?"

Terrance could not pin down the exact day, but he remembered running into William and his friend Edward at the Barren Bull pub about a week before his father died.

"What was this Edward's last name?" Oren asked.

"I'm quite sure it was Keith. I believe he was also related to William's girl friend, Lenora."

"Do you know Lenora's last name?"

"No, but I know she works in the library office at Mulready School."

"Thank you, Mr. Duncombe. Now, if you can recommend a place to stay for tonight, that should do it. I'll make my inquires tomorrow and then stop by to see you before I return to London."

Terrance suggested the Clyde Hotel on Findley Street and offered to have one of his men take him to the hotel.

"Say, I do remember something else," Terrance said, as Oren was about to leave. "Yes, I seem to remember that Edward Keith was from Chester. This Lenora may have been too."

"Thanks, that will help, and I will see you tomorrow."

Oren Eflow's first stop after his typically substantial breakfast was at Mulready School. He learned that Lenora's last name was Franklin and that she resigned her position two weeks previously.

The head schoolmistress at Mulready said that Lenora had seemed ill for several days before she left her position. She added that Lenora was a fine young lady and she missed her.

Oren's next stop was the Barren Bull. He talked to Simon Jones the proprietor and learned that William and Edward Keith were often in the pub, but neither Jones nor any of the other help had seen either of them for a while.

"You might come back tonight and ask Spencer, he's on most nights," said Jones.

"Thanks, I will."

Oren's next stop was William's residence. It was locked.

He'd learned from Terrance that a woman named Ethel Prentise cleaned William's place and he'd gotten her address from Terrance, so he went there next. The Prentise place was on Flint Street and he found it without much difficulty, but no one answered his ring. As it was time for lunch, he made his way back to the Barren Bull. As he walked, he thought to himself that he didn't really know what William did for a living. Terrance had never mentioned it, and he had never asked. After his meal, he hailed a carriage and returned to Pulteney Publishing. Terrance was still in his office.

"Mr. Eflow, so soon?"

"Well, yes, I needed to ask you a few more questions."

He took a chair and continued. "What is your brother's employment?"

"He's been out of work for some time. He did receive an inheritance from our mother, and father sent a small amount every month. Also, I believe he had made application to teach at Mulready School, whether he got the job, I don't know."

"Mulready," said Oren. "That's where Lenora Franklin worked."

"Franklin. That's what her last name was. I remember now.

Quite attractive, as I recall, too," said Terrance. "And you say, worked. Is she not there anymore?"

"No, she's not. Gave her notice about two weeks ago. I guess that's it for now. I'm going to go see if I can talk to Ethel Prentise."

A woman, whom he assumed must be Ethel Prentise, opened the door when he rang. She was, he guessed, some-where in her fifties. Her gray hair seemed to stick out in all directions and her heavy smock showed the dirt of her profession. She likely had just returned home.

He introduced himself and told her his reasons for wanting to ask her some questions. She was hesitant at first. Then she invited him in, and without any prodding by Oren, told him of her concerns about her employer and her distrust of the man, Edward Keith and finally, about the steamer trunk.

"And you say that this Edward Keith has been living in Mr. Duncombe's flat for some time?"

"Yes. And he told me yesterday that the rent was paid through the end of the month and then he would be leaving."

"Did he say where he is going?"

"No, and I didn't ask and I really don't care," she said, indifferently.

"Tell me more about the incident with the trunk," Oren said. She needed little encouragement.

She once again related how rude Edward Keith had been and then her dismay when she returned to find not only the trunk gone, but to learn that Mr. Duncombe was gone too.

"And you remember that the name on the trunk tag was either Dunlap or Duncan?"

"I'm fairly sure it was Duncan, the more I think about it."

"But you can't remember whether the tag had a destination name on it?"

"No, not for sure, but I remember something about *Black* or *Blackman*, or words similar to that," she said, now beginning to show signs of impatience, as if looking for a way out.

"Thank you Mrs. Prentise, you've helped me quite a bit."

He rose, thanked her for her time and information and left his card, saying that if she thought of anything else to contact him through Terrance Duncombe.

As he started walking up Flint Street to where he'd left his carriage, she called out his name. "I do remember something else. There were letters *S S* in front of the name that had *Black* in it."

That night he returned to the Barren Bull, but learned nothing more from the night barman, Spencer. He left the pub and as he'd returned his carriage earlier, began walking back to the Clyde Hotel. He sensed, then heard someone following him. He stopped, turned and the man almost walked right into him. The man stumbled and his Bowler fell on the walk. He appeared to be about Oren's age, mostly bald, slightly shorter and very smartly dressed. As he didn't appear to be the criminal sort, Oren relaxed, reached down with some effort, and retrevied the hat.

"Here, you dropped this," Oren said.

"Thank you." He extended his hand. "My name is Stanton Beasly. I overheard you asking about William Duncombe, but I didn't want to talk inside."

"You know him?" asked Oren.

"Yes."

"Do you know where he is?"

"No, but I need to find him, too," said Beasly.

"Perhaps we'd better talk then, but not here in the cold. I'm staying just up the street at the Clyde."

The hotel had a small parlor near the front desk. It was deserted at the late hour, so Oren and Beasly had the room to themselves.

Oren spoke first, explaining his reasons for trying to locate William, but not revealing much of what he'd already learned. The hotel night man appeared and Oren asked if they might have a Brandy. He nodded yes and left to get the drinks. Beasly didn't wait for the Brandy to start his explanation.

"You see, I'm the assistant bank manager at Barclays in Chester, and four months ago, I approved a small loan for a business venture of Mr. Duncombe's here in Bath."

The drinks arrived and Oren signed the slip of paper and gave the man five pence. *After all, the Duncombe's can afford it*, he thought.

"Go on, Mr. Beasly."

"Well, the note was due to be paid two weeks ago."

Beasly went on to explain that William had not answered his two letters of inquiry. He came to Bath two days ago and had learned nothing. Tonight was his last night and he just happened to be at the pub and overheard Oren talking to the barman.

"Do you know a man named Edward Keith?" Oren asked.

"Why, yes, he was with Mr. Duncombe when he came to get the bank draft and I understood that he might be involved in Duncombe's business venture, but in what capacity, it was never explained."

Beasly rambled on for another few minutes and it became obvious to Oren that the loan approval had been based solely on the Duncombe name, with no collateral, and now Mr. Beasly's neck was stuck out a bit too far.

Should he tell him more of what he had learned?

"Stanton, I really can't add much more. As I've told you, the Duncombe family hired me to find William. If I learn anything that can help you, I'll contact you."

Beasly reached in his vest pocket. "Here's my card. Thank you for your time. I'm just up the street at the Gilbert Hotel and my train leaves early. So thanks again and goodnight."

As Beasly walked away, Oren rethought what he had learned. Yes, he now had one reason for William's unavailability and perhaps his hasty departure. And this Keith person. His name keeps popping up all the time.

What a strange set of circumstances, he thought. *Two more things to do tomorrow. Try and find this Edward Keith and, as he was sure that the S S must be part of a ship's name, he would travel to the nearest ports, South Hampton and Portsmouth, and make inquires.*

His inquires the next day concerning Edward Keith turned up no new information. The lady in the neighboring flat told him that Mr. Keith had not been around for several days. He caught a carriage for the station and boarded the 10:16 to South Hampton.

As it turned out, Oren didn't continue on to Portsmouth. In South Hampton he learned more than enough to answer many of his questions. He returned to Bath with what he believed were many of the answers to the whereabouts of William Duncombe.

He still wished to confront Edward Keith, but for now, he was satisfied he had most of the story.

The next morning, Oren rose early, checked out of his room and hired a carriage to take him to the office of Terrance Duncombe. He arrived at Pulteney Publishing precisely at nine and was promptly shown in. Terrance rose as Oren entered.

"Mr. Eflow, good morning. I trust you have some useful information for me," Terrance said.

"Yes, I believe I do."

Over the next several minutes Oren related what he had learned in Bath and South Hampton and then speculated a series of events culminating in William's departure from England. He learned that a vessel the *S S Blackadder* sailed from South Hampton on October 12. The trunk seen by Mrs. Prentise was most likely shipped to South Hampton for transport on that vessel. William's rumored lady friend, one Miss Lenora Franklin, was on the passenger list of the *Blackadder*. William's residence was currently occupied by an Edward Keith. The same Edward Keith that had been present when Mrs. Prentise discovered the trunk. Oren reasoned that the person's name seen on the shipping label was most likely a false name for William. In fact, he had noted on the passenger list a Benjamin Duncan from Chester. A purser's note indicated that a trunk consigned from Bath was to be placed in Mr. Duncan's cabin. Finally, he learned that the rent on William's residence was paid till the end of October. He decided to leave out what he'd learned from Stanton Beasly, for the time being.

"I still want to talk to Edward Keith, but for now, that's it," Oren said.

"And you say the ship was bound for New York?"

"Yes, New York."

New York City

Michael O'Toole's place was on 10th Street and like most of the other rooms in the tenements in Greenwich Village, it was small, rundown and barely livable, but it was cheap rent. His room was on the fourth floor and he and Ben struggled to carry the steamer trunk up the narrow flight of stairs. Martha and Lenora gave them encouragement, but stayed out of their way. After washing up, they all climbed in the wagon and headed up 10th to Delaware and Martha's apartment building.

The condition of the neighborhood on Delaware was substantially better than where Sean and Michael lived. In fact, several blocks north of Martha's building there was a district of single family residences. The Roosevelt house took up most of one block. Before getting her job at Hunter College, Martha interviewed for a tutoring position for the Roosevelt's son Theodore. She didn't get the job, but had met young Mr. Roosevelt and was fascinated by his tales of adventure in the Dakota Territories. Even though he was only twelve at the time, he seemed sure that he would one day become a cowboy in the Dakotas.

"Here's our building," Martha said.

Martha's room was on the first floor and, in no time, Michael and Ben had Lenora's trunk inside. Ben said he would accompany Michael back to the stables where he rented the wagon. The sisters were alone. Lenora removed her coat and, for the first time, Martha noticed her sister had put on some weight.

"So now that we're alone, what's all the mystery about?" said Martha.

"What do you mean, mystery?"

"Come on, you know what I mean. You said in your letter in September that you were going to leave Chester. Then in the letter I got two weeks ago, you said you and William were thinking of coming to America. Then I get the telegram from our cousin Edward that you were arriving in New York today and telling me about William using a different name. And you say, 'what mystery'."

"I'm sorry, Martha, it all happened so fast," Lenora said.

"And why the rush to get married?" Martha asked. "He's a handsome fellow, I have to admit, but you could have waited until you got here."

Lenora moved away from the trunk and sat on the bed. Martha could see the tears running down her cheeks and was sorry she'd been so rough on her sister. She sat next to Lenora and put her arm around her. For several minutes they just sat there. Then slowly, and almost in a whisper, Lenora told Martha the story of her and William's romance, William's troubles with his business debts and then finally the main reason for their hasty departure and marriage at sea.

Chapter Eight

The lamps in the room were turned down low, except for the teal peg lamp on the dressing table that illuminated a single sheet of stationary. After several hours today and each of the preceding nights since leaving London, unraveling the riddle had become an obsession. A stack of unused notepaper lay on the bed, and the floor was covered with dozens of crumpled sheets. Since sneaking into the living room at the Duncombe house and taking the paper with the words, there had been but one objective. Solve the puzzle and find the treasure. *I deserve it after all I've been through,* was the constant thought.

Finally the answer was there. It was so simple. There was just one problem. The missing postage labels. Without those, the central part of the riddle was missing. Six letters that filled in the gap and likely spelled at least one or two words. The same thoughts kept repeating. *The family was due to meet in a few days at the barrister's office in London. There wasn't much time. Maybe William will show up and the puzzle will be solved. Then my advantage will be lost.*

Terrance was the first to arrive, followed shortly by James and Giles. When ten minutes passed with no sign of Mary, Malcolm offered them a drink and cigars from the humidor on his desk. Another ten minutes passed and Giles and James refreshed their drinks. When Mary arrived a few minutes later, the room was thick with smoke, so much so that Mary immediately requested Malcolm to open his office window.

"Mary," Giles said, "why don't you try one of Malcolm's good Cubans and relax."

She ignored her brother's gibe and, raising her large bussle, took the remaining seat in the office. "No thank you, but I will have a glass of Sherry. It looks like I need to catch up with the rest of you."

"Where's Tyler? Did you leave him to mind the store and take care of Olivia?" James asked, quite noticeably feeling the effects of two glasses of scotch.

"Never mind, brother, and I suggest you taper off on your drinking. We've got some serious work ahead," Mary said.

James rose and bowed to Mary. "Very well, sis."

Malcolm watched the interplay between the siblings with some amusement. *Maybe Giles had been right*, he thought, *this whole thing may bring them together after all.* He cleared his throat to get their attention.

"First we need to sign these papers. Then I'd like to hear where you stand on solving the puzzle, and James, I'd especially like to hear what you and Terrance have learned about William's whereabouts."

"Yes," said Mary, and then turning to James, "we would all like to hear that, and for your information James, Tyler had some pressing business at the mill, or otherwise he would have been here for our meeting."

James nodded and raised his glass. "Touché."

The signing of the documents took only a few minutes and

then James and Terrance told them what the investigator had found out about William. For a moment no one spoke, then Mary broke the silence.

"He's gone to America!"

"Very likely," said James.

"Do we know whether he got father's letter or the telegram?" asked Giles.

"No, but we have to assume he did," said Terrance. "This Keith fellow that Mr. Eflow hasn't located as yet, may be able to shed some light on that question."

"Can we contact him in America?" Mary asked.

"I'm already working on that, Mary," said James. "I've sent a telegram to our agents in New York and asked them to contact the owners of the *Blackadder*, John Willis & Sons, and find out as much as they can. Willis is primarily a passenger carrier, but we've worked with them before on a cargo shipment and know several of their New York people."

"So for now that's all we can do as far as William is concerned," said Terrance. "In the meantime, what has anyone come up with regarding our riddle."

"I'm not done talking about William, Terrance," Mary said, and went on. "How about this investigator, Eflow, can't we have him keep working on this. Find this Keith person?"

"He will, Mary, and as soon as he has anything to report, I'll follow up on it and let you all know," said James. "Now, as Terrance has suggested, let's see what we have on the riddle. How about you, Giles, any new ideas?"

By Mary's body language James could tell that Mary was not satisfied. *She's getting to be her typical big pain*, he thought. *Just like when we were children.*

Giles, too, could tell his sister was not satisfied, but pressed on. "Yes, I think I have a solution to at least part of the puzzle," he said.

That got everyone's attention, including Mary.

"You see," Giles said, "there has to be some primary element that makes sense in the riddle. A key, so to speak. Mary, you're probably too young to remember this, but James and Terrance will. Remember the time father gave us that nonsense riddle where the last letter of each word spelled other words."

"I remember that," said James.

Terrance nodded.

Giles went on. "Now look closely."

He held out a piece of paper with the now familiar words, arranged in the order of the letter positions on the postal stamps. First row AA through AF, then row BA though BF, DA through DF and finally EA through EF. He had circled several words. They were *First, Eden's, Eve, First* and *One.*

"I believe that in this riddle, the first letter of each word forms a word in the riddle," Giles said.

"By God, I think Giles has got it," said Terrance. "Look, the first letter of the first four words spells YORK."

In no time, they were each trying to form the rest of the message and Malcolm was caught up in the task, too. Giles had already formed what he believed were the correct words and put them in order, assuming the words that were capitalized started a sentence. The rest would soon come to the same conclusion he did, that without the missing row, CA through CF, the full meaning of the riddle would escape them. He presumed this much: the treasure must most likely be hidden at the family farm in York.

"Well, it's obvious that we need to find William, or at least the letter that was sent to him," James said.

"Unless, of course, Malcolm wants to open his little safe and save us the effort," said Mary.

Here she was, once more in his arms. She'd told herself no over and over again, but when the letter arrived saying he'd be in London tonight, she couldn't resist. This time, however, she had reasons beyond just the physical pleasure to be with him, so she relented without much argument. Having Henry sleeping in the next room was a bit awkward, but they'd dealt with that before.

She could tell by his breathing that he was getting close, so she stopped thinking about her other motives and surrendered herself to the pure pleasure she always felt when they made love.

Terrance was usually not much for affection afterwards, but this night he rolled onto his side, keeping her locked in his embrace. "Thank you for agreeing to see me," he whispered.

"I guess I just can't resist," she said, somewhat mockingly, but knowing it was true. She really wanted to get up and talk about the family meeting today and whether they had collectively gotten any closer to solving the riddle. His hands started exploring again and she could feel him come alive against her. *Time to move, if I'm going to,* she thought.

"Terry, I need to get up, and we need to talk."

Reluctantly he let his arms relax and rolled away. "All right, but come back to bed." He gave her a pat on the rear as she sat up and walked to the toilet.

She returned wearing her robe and holding two glasses. "Some scotch?"

"All right, thanks," he said. "So what's this we need to discuss. I know that we agreed not to see each other, but I just couldn't help it."

"What do you mean, we agreed. You're the one who broke it off, Terry. But, that's not it. I wanted to know about your meeting today. Have you found William and did you solve any more of the puzzle in the letters?"

He told her what they'd learned about William and about how Giles had stumbled onto the possible key to solving the location of the inheritance treasure. What Giles had discovered, she had already figured out and what Terrance related to her, confirmed her conclusions. *So, I was right. But without the other words from Williams's letter, the location was, at best, a guess. But a guess worth pursuing.*

Soon Terrance tired of the conversation and pulled her closer to the bed, undoing the tie on her robe at the same time. "There, that's more like it. Enough talk."

She had probably learned all there was to learn, so she let his soft, demanding hands once again break down what resistance she had.

The next day Terrance met again with Giles, James and Mary at Malcolm Jones' office on Baker Street in London. James reported that he met with Oren Eflow earlier and asked him to keep looking for Edward Keith. Nothing had been heard yet from their New York agents regarding William. As they had concluded that the inheritance treasure likely was located in York, and probably at the farm, they decided to meet again in a week at Giles and Ruth's house in York. They all agreed to keep working on the riddle, trying to figure out the missing words that tied the first and last parts together. Malcolm walked them to the door and shook hands each of their hands.

"After today, I don't believe I can add much to your quest, so I wish you gook luck," he said.

When James returned to his office the next morning there was a message from Oren Eflow. He was catching the 10:40 to Chester from Charing Cross station. If after two days of inquires he hadn't found Edward Keith, he would then go to Bath one more time before returning to London.

What Oren didn't say in the note was that while in Chester he would contact Stanton Beasly to see if he couldn't find out a little more about William's business venture.

The Chester Train Station was near the Abbottsford Court Hotel, so Oren decided to walk. He hadn't been in Chester for some time, but it was his second most favorite city, behind York. Besides his love of gardening, Oren had a passion for English history and, had he not ended up a police inspector, he would have surely pursued some career that involved the study of the ancient beginnings of England. The hotel was near the site of the old harbor and at the end of one of the sections of Rows. The Rows were one of the most distinctive features of Chester and dated back to the 14th century. These were double-level walkways with shops at both street level and on the first floors. Barclays' Bank was on the street level section that fronted Liverpool Road. Oren planned to visit Mr. Beasly at Barclays' once he registered at the Abbottsford.

He found Stanton Beasly in his office, near the rear of the bank.

"Good afternoon, Stanton. I appreciate you seeing me on such short notice."

"No, my pleasure. If you can help me find Mr. Duncombe

you will have helped me immensely."

"I have some rather bad news for you on that score, I'm afraid," said Oren. He went on to explain that he was sure that William had sailed for America, and the chances of locating him were next to impossible. The Duncombe family was aware of this, but Oren had not yet informed them of William's financial problems. He would, after a thorough explanation. For Beasly's benefit, he suggested the family might consider restitution if circumstances warranted. He could tell from Beasly's reaction that he was relieved.

"Do you intend to try and find him in America?" Beasly asked.

"That will be up to the family, but I doubt it," he said. "There is a matter, though, that you can help with that may determine what they do next, and that concerns this Edward Keith."

"As I told you in Bath, I only met him twice and that was here at the bank with Mr. Duncombe."

"Did he sign the loan papers?" Beasly shook his head.

"But you sensed that he was part of the venture."

"Yes, I did."

"How much was the loan?"

"Two hundred pounds."

"Do you have any idea where Keith lived in Chester?"

"No, but I heard them twice mention his cousin's place on Walpole Lane."

Oren left the bank after a few more questions, but it was obvious that Beasly knew less about Edward Keith than he did. He assured Beasly that he would keep him informed, but knew that he'd probably served his purpose and really doubted whether the Duncombes would repay the two hundred pound debt. He would tell them about it now, however, as it had to be the reason William fled England.

Yet the more he thought about it, two hundred pounds seemed hardly enough to motivate fleeing the country.

Oren spent the rest of the day making inquires about Lenora Franklin and Edward Keith. Walpole Lane was one of the shorter sections of the Rows, but still contained some thirty to forty shops and Inns, so it was slow going. He visited about half the shops and then returned to his hotel for dinner. That night he reflected that, so far, he had learned nothing.

By mid morning the next day, he was even more discouraged and then he saw the sign. *"Franklin Fabrics."*

He was surprised at how busy the shop was. Three ladies were picking through bolts of material and a fourth was having her purchase wrapped by an older woman behind the counter. As he was observing this, a man emerged from the rear of the shop with a bolt of material.

"I found this wool with the tartan pattern, Mrs. Winston." He walked over to the lady nearest Oren.

"Thank you, Mr. Franklin. That looks like what I need. I'll take three yards."

He set the bolt down and, smiling, looked in Oren's direction.

"I'll be with you as soon as I can, Sir," he said.

The lady behind the counter took the bolt from Mr. Franklin and rolled out the material on the counter.

"Now, how may I help you?" he asked Oren.

Oren introduced himself and then asked the question he'd been waiting to ask. "Are you perhaps related to a Miss Lenora Franklin?"

The woman behind the counter dropped her scissors. "Oh, Clarence, I knew something was wrong."

Edward had been following Oren Eflow all morning and once he saw him go into his aunt and uncle's shop, he figured it was time to bid a hasty retreat. He planned to leave Chester tomorrow anyway, but was curious to see this man who had been making inquires about him and Lenora. Spencer at the Barren Bull in Bath had described the man and Edward was sure this was the same person. He'd paid Spencer dearly for the information and the promise not to tell anything about him. Then late yesterday, his friend Evan, who worked at the Abbottsford, told him about a heavyset man staying there who was asking questions about him. He learned the man's name was Eflow and his description fit the one of the man from Bath. He knew about Beasly's inquires in Bath too, so he assumed that Eflow was in someone else's employment rather than the Barclay Bank. *But who*, he thought. *And why all the interest in William? It had to be expensive to hire someone to make these inquires. William had been such an easy mark and convincing him to leave for America had been so simple. He hadn't counted on Lenora and William falling in love, but in the end, it had been to his advantage. He was planning to leave for Edinburgh tomorrow, but perhaps he'd delay it a day or so and see what this fellow Eflow was up to.*

Edward backed away from his hiding place and waited for Oren's appearance.

Inside the fabric shop, Oren was assuring the Franklins that as far as he knew their daughter was just fine. They told him of the letter she left for them the morning she had gone. All it said was that she was leaving and would write them when she arrived at her destination.

They were Lenora's parents, and their reaction when he next asked about Edward Keith was surprising. "Is he involved in Lenora's leaving?" said Mr. Franklin. Mrs. Franklin shook her head in disgust and looked at Oren.

"I hope not, he's rotten through and through." she said. "He's part of the reason our other daughter, Martha, left last year. She's in America now."

When the customers left the shop, they continued talking about Lenora and Martha. Oren became more convinced that Lenora had gone to America with William Duncombe, but he didn't express his conclusion to the Franklins. Oren assured the Franklins, however, that he would write them if he learned anything positive about their daughter. They in turn, told him they would write him when they received a letter from Lenora. When he asked about whether they knew a William Duncombe, they both said no. As to the whereabouts of Edward Keith, they also were not able to help. They did relate to Oren how Edward had once worked for them and they let him go after discovering he was taking money from the cash box. They also had heard that he had been in some business venture in Bath that failed. They further believed that Edward had once taken a more than plutonic interest in Martha and they constantly warned Lenora about associating with Edward. They suspected, however from her letter, that she spent time with him in Bath. Finally, just a few days ago, they received a letter from a solicitor in Bath asking for information about Edward.

"Did you answer the letter?"

Clarence replied, "No."

"May I see it?" asked Oren.

The letter was from Hanby & Soltise, Solicitors, and indicated that Edward was to contact them regarding the *River Dee Spa Company, Ltd.*. The letter was signed by a Mr. Silas Hanby.

Just as Edward was about to give up, Oren walked out of the shop door accompanied by Clarence Franklin. *There's that bastard Clarence,* he thought. He pressed back into the opening as far as he could, so as not to be seen. He could hear them exchanging their good-byes.

"Yes, I'm going to go to Bath tomorrow for one final check, and then see Terrance Duncombe before returning to London."

"Have a safe trip, Mr. Eflow, and be sure to let us know if you hear anything about Lenora."

Edward tried to remember something William had told him about his brother. *Oh yes, now he remembered. Terrance was the one whom William said was having an affair with some seamstress in London. Perhaps he'll just follow this Mr. Eflow back to Bath and see what develops. Something's going on here.*

He waited while Eflow went laboriously down the stairs to the street level, and then followed.

Oren got to Terrance's office at nine, but the secretary said Mr. Duncombe was meeting with a paper supplier and couldn't see him until noon. She handed Oren a note in which Terrance suggested they meet at eleven-thirty for lunch at a place called the Heston Grill. Oren used the intervening time to call on Mr. Silas Hanby at his law office. After introducing himself he learned that Edward Keith and William Duncombe purchased land near one of Bath's natural hot springs. A down payment had been made, but no funds had been received since. They used Hanby to draw up the contract.

Edward Keith then borrowed funds, using the land as collateral. The note was due on the land and the bank was inquiring about the monies they had lent. Hanby informed Oren that in addition to the letter he sent to Chester, he also had written Mr. Terrance Duncombe in Bath. Mr. Hanby was not at all pleased when Oren related to him what he knew about Edward Keith and that he was sure that William Duncombe had left England.

Oren arrived at the Heston Grill to find Terrance waiting for him. He was seated in one of the booths by the windows.

"So, bring me up to date," said Terrance, after they had exchanged pleasantries and placed their order.

Oren told him of his trip to Chester and his conversation with the Franklins and then about his meeting earlier with Mr. Hanby.

"Yes, I got the letter from Hanby yesterday," said Terrance. "What a mess. I'll wager that Edward Keith is long gone by now. Do you think he may have sailed with William and Lenora Franklin?"

"I don't know, but I doubt it. I think he duped your brother. The Franklins led me to believe he's always been a bit of a scoundrel," said Oren.

"Do you think William ever got the telegram from Malcolm Jones and the letter from my father?"

"I doubt that too. If he had, I'm sure he wouldn't have left England for America. His inheritance and his part of the hidden treasure would pay many times over what his debts are."

"Just think, his letter is most likely the key to solving the riddle regarding the location of the treasure left by my father," said Terrance.

"Yes," said Oren. "Who knows where that letter is? He may have not seen it or laid it aside unopened in his haste."

Edward Keith tipped the hostess dearly for giving him the booth next to Terrance. Terrance had never met him and he trusted that Eflow would not be looking for him in this setting. Hopefully, he appeared as just another luncheon guest. Even so, he sat on the side of the booth that would put him behind Terrance and not visible by someone sitting opposite. In his position, he could hear everything that was being said.

The letter. Yes, he remembered it, and the telegram too. What an idiot. He should have opened it, but he'd been too eager to get William's things to him in South Hampton. Where had he put them? Oh yes, he remembered. A hidden treasure with a riddle in the letter. Damn! What was he saying now?

"I'm going to London tomorrow and then on to York to meet with the family. Are you returning today?"

"Yes," said Oren. "I'll report to James and then I don't see what else I can contribute. I've just about given up on finding this Keith."

"Very well," said Terrance.

They made idle conversation for a few more minutes and then said their good-byes. Eflow departed first, followed by Terrance.

Edward Keith paid his bill and left shortly thereafter. As he made his way to his hotel he wondered to himself how he could take advantage of this new information. *Should he follow Eflow? Follow Terrance Duncombe to London? Would William write to him? It was now Ben Duncan, he remembered. Or should he just forget the whole thing and go to Cardiff, as had been his original plan? He had the money he'd bilked from William and the others, safely hidden away, and it would be plenty for a new start in Canada. There was still time to change his schedule and go through London. He had to admit that this acting like a spy was quite exciting.*

London, England, December – 1872

The Fire Brigade from London Station #1 was the first on the scene and the Brigades from Stations #2 and #3 quickly joined them. They were too late.

The *Times* reported the next day that an entire block of buildings on Fenchurch Street had been lost. Only two deaths were reported, that of a leading London barrister, Malcolm Jones and a solicitor from Jones' office, one Julius Nithdale. Another solicitor, one Lawton Milton, said that the fire started when a lamp was knocked over. Apparently Mr. Jones and Mr. Nithdale tried to put out the fire, but it spread quickly, trapping them inside. Mr. Milton escaped with minor injuries.

Yorkshire, England, May – 1874

An earthquake is very unusual for England, so the magnitude of the one that shook Yorkshire was even more surprising. The *York Daily Post* reported that several buildings were damaged severely and would require extensive repair.

Chicago, Illinois, July -- 1874

Gold is discovered in the Dakota Territory.

The Chicago Tribune reported on July 30th that surveyors with General Custer's expedition discovered gold in the Black Hills area.

Part Two

1907

*"Do not bring every man into your home,
    for many are the wiles of the crafty."*

*"Like a decoy partridge in a cage, so is the mind
    of a proud man, and like a spy he observes your
    weakness;
for he lies in wait, turning good into evil,
    and to worthy actions he will attach blame."*

Sirach 11:29-31

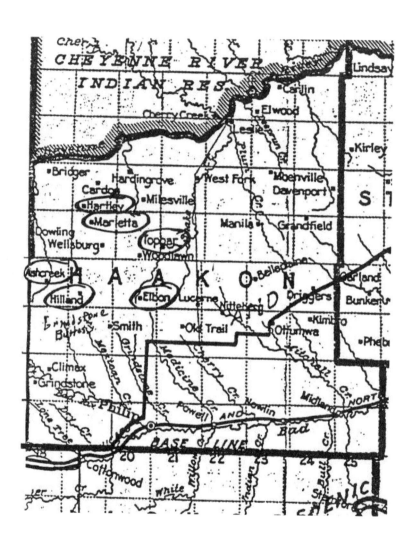

Haakon County – Stanley County, South Dakota
Early 1900's

Chapter Nine

The funeral was attended by most of the farmers and ranchers in Stanley County and the tiny Community Church in Ash Creek was packed. The August heat was unbearable and Paul Blanton, sweating profusely under his clerical collar, did his best to keep the service short. At the conclusion, he announced there would be a graveside service and then everyone was invited to a luncheon at the Duncan place.

Will and Chester Duncan, Frank and Leonard O'Toole and their father Mickey, the Herrman brothers and Jesse Mason hefted the casket and made their way up the short path to the cemetery. Lenora walked just behind the pallbearers, arm in arm with her daughter Lila. Martha O'Toole, her daughter Elizabeth and Pastor Blanton lead the rest of the procession.

The injuries from the thrasher accident had been horrendous, so there was no viewing. Chester was there when it happened and tried to prevent his mother from seeing his dad's broken body. However, fifteen years of life on the prairie and thirty-five years of marriage steeled her resolve and Lenora had her few minutes with Ben before the coffin was sealed. At the graveside service, Lenora again asked for some time alone.

Goodbye Ben. I'll always love you.

They came to the Dakotas in 1892. Willard was twenty, Chester eighteen, and Lila sixteen. Ben wanted to leave Alton with Mickey in '77 when the Dakota gold rush fever got the best of him, but instead, he heeded Lenora's advice and stayed in Illinois. Mickey didn't find gold, but earned enough by cooking in the mining camps near Deadwood to buy a place in Lead and send for Martha and the children.

The day Martha and the children left to join Mickey was one of the saddest days in Lenora's life. Since that first day in New York, they'd been inseparable. When she and Ben moved to Alton in 1875, Martha and Mickey had followed within four months, even though Martha was five months pregnant with Elizabeth. Those three years in Alton had been wonderful.

Over the years, both sisters kept in touch with their parents in Chester. Martha had regularly written her mother since she arrived in America, but only after much encouragement did Lenora start writing home. Lenora's first letter told of her marriage to Ben Duncan and the impending birth of their child. She also explained to the Franklins that her husband had financial problems that prompted them to leave secretly. She did not reveal that her husband, Ben Duncan, was in fact William Duncombe. Lastly, she asked her parents not to impart to others any of the information. She did not mention Edward Keith and his involvement with her husband.

Lenora and Martha started the routine of writing to each other at least once a month. Martha's letters always closed with words of encouragement to come and join them in South Dakota, but Ben's small farm near Alton was providing them with a steady income and Lenora didn't want to uproot the children.

When Lenora saw the book, *The Winning of the West*, by their New York friend, Teddy Roosevelt, she bought it and after reading it herself, sent it to Martha. Lenora recalled the tales of the Dakotas told to her in New York by their young friend Teddy, and she had to admit, that she'd always dreamed of one day going west. Her dreams soon became reality.

The drought of 1891 ruined most of the farmers in Illinois and it hit the Duncans hard. They held onto the house and half the land, but lost everything else. So in 1892, three years after South Dakota became a state, they sold their small farm and headed west to join the O'Tooles.

It was the first time Chester and Lila had been on a train, so the two teenagers were excited about everything they saw out the car windows. Willard was not happy about leaving his girlfriend. Sheila Wilson was in her second year at Shurtleff College near Alton. By the time they arrived in Pierre, however, he too was caught up in the excitement of their adventure. Ben and Lenora were secretly glad that Willard would be away from Sheila. Shurtleff was a very fashionable school for well-to-do girls and Lenora was convinced that the class differences between Shelia and Willard were too great to overcome for any long-term relationship.

The railway line ended in Pierre and the rest of their trip would be by wagon. After Ben got everyone settled into two rooms at the Capitol Hotel on Main Street, he and Willard started their search for a team and wagon. They made the best deal they could on two Percheron draft horses and then returned to the train station to get the rest of their belongings. The first to be loaded was Ben's steamer trunk. Ben had tried to get Lenora to leave it in Illinois, but she said it had been with them from the start and she couldn't part with it now.

To get to Lead, they would first have to cross the Missouri River and then travel nearly 250 miles. The money they had remaining after the hotel bill and purchase of the wagon and team would barely cover the barge fee and buy them sufficient provisions for the trip. In Martha's last letter she said that Mickey found a job for both Willard and Ben at the mine in Lead and they could stay with them until they found their own place.

After crossing the Missouri to Fort Pierre, they traveled almost due west for seven days, following the Bad River. When they crossed the Cheyenne River, they headed northwest toward Deadwood and Lead. The last day of the trip proved to be their worst. From their campsite near Rapid City, they had to climb over 2000 feet to reach Lead and the road was not much improved since the miners first used it in 1876. They had to stop once to repair a wheel and two more times to rest the horses, which Lila had named Major and Colonel. In all, it took an extra day, but finally they arrived at Martha and Mickey's place on Lagg Street.

Despite the admonishments of his parents, Willard left Lead two years later and returned to Alton to marry Sheila. He'd never been completely happy, especially living with his family, and the work in the mine was taking a toll on his health. Willard proposed to Sheila when he visited Alton in the summer of 1893.

The following year, Chester married Jane Herrman. They moved to Stanley County where her parents had a cattle ranch with prime grazing land, near the Cheyenne River. Both the Duncans and the O'Tooles went to the wedding. Lila was thrilled when Jane asked her to be maid of honor.

Willard returned to be his brother's best man, but Sheila stayed in Alton, as she was pregnant with their first child. The Duncan children were a handsome lot. Willard, now twenty-two, resembled his father, but was several inches taller, inheriting that characteristic from Lenora's side. He had dark hair which, even at his young age, was beginning to thin. Chester was shorter and stockier than his older brother. Lenora had never met Ben's father, but from his description, Chester sounded like a carbon copy, especially his usual thoughtful expression and dry wit. Lila looked just like her mother: light complexioned, auburn hair, always smiling and though petite, very shapely. Now at eighteen, in a town where the ratio of men to women was very lopsided, her suitors were many. Too many for Ben's liking.

The mines fell on hard times in 1902. The Duncans and the O'Tooles, already tired of their life in Lead, decided their future lay further east, closer to their children. Both Chester, and Lila, who'd married Jesse Mason had moved north of Philip. They wrote that large sections of land were available near them as part of the Homestead Act. After much vacillation over the pros and cons of homesteading, the O'Tooles and Duncans decided to move east. The day they left Lead, Ben suggested they'd have more room in the wagon if they didn't take his steamer trunk. Lenora said no.

Quarter sections, about 160 acres, were selling for $1.25 an acre. Neither family had saved much, but with what they had, plus the income from selling their homes, each came up with the $2000 needed. The other conditions of homesteading in South Dakota were digging a well, fencing in the land and living there for a minimum of eight months. So, in March of 1902, Ben and Mickey filed a deed at the land office in Philip.

"Mom, here's some tea," said Lila. "Twinings, your favorite."

She put the cup on the table and sat next to her mother. "Come on, have a few sips."

"Are they all gone?" Lenora asked.

"All but Aunt Martha and Jane. Uncle Mickey, Jesse, Chester and Will are out in the barn doing the chores."

Lenora took a few sips and turned to Lila. "Too bad Sheila and the children couldn't come with Willard."

"Yes, but they are pretty young for such a long trip, Mom."

"I guess so," she said pensively, taking another sip.

Life on the prairie had weathered Lenora's skin and the last few days had taken their toll both physically and mentally. She looked old beyond her years. Then, as if she'd just had a revelation, the tension left her face. She rose, turned and smiled at her daughter. "All right, let's get this mess cleared up."

Life slowly returned to some semblance of routine for the next three months. Chester and Jesse helped with the cattle and Mickey and Leonard O'Toole got the winter wheat crop planted. Lila rode over often to check on her mom, who to her, seemed to be just going through the paces with only a few signs of her normal, happy disposition.

The Masons farmed 320 acres east of Lenora's place, on Bridges Creek. They built their house in an area surrounded by trees that offered shade and refuge, in sharp contrast to the bleakness of the prairie. Mickey and Martha's farm was a few miles south, closer to Hilland. Those first two weeks after the funeral, Martha visited often. Lenora jokingly said that she was only coming to help her eat up all the food left by the church ladies.

Since Lenora and Martha had been together, they'd always shared the holiday dinners, with Martha doing Thanksgiving and Lenora, Christmas. So as usual, Martha invited everyone to the O'Toole place for the turkey dinner. She and Mickey were concerned about how Lenora would do on her first Thanksgiving in thirty-five years without Ben. When everyone heard from Willard that he, Sheila and the boys were coming, whatever fears they had about Lenora were set aside. Lenora was ecstatic and was like her old self again.

During dinner, Lila brought up the subject of Christmas, but before anyone could get a word in, Lenora announced that everyone was invited to her place. She said she'd always had Christmas and this year was not going to be an exception. Lila, however was just as stubborn as her mother, and only agreed if she and Jane could help with the dinner and getting the house ready.

Lila and Jane arrived the day before Christmas, as promised. They shushed Lenora into the kitchen and started cleaning everything in sight. Lila didn't bring up the question of her dad's things. It had been on her mind and she was hoping to find the right time to mention it. That evening, when Jane went to use the outhouse and get some wood for the stove, and Lila and her mom were in the kitchen cleaning and stuffing the turkey, she broached the subject.

"Mom, the only thing we didn't do today was go through Dad's closet and his bureau and get into the attic."

At first Lenora seemed not to hear her daughter. Lila sensed, however, that her mother was struggling with an answer and wished she'd waited until another time. Then she looked up, smiled and nodded.

"Thanks, honey. I guess I just needed a good prod."

They decided that just the two of them would go through Ben's things and Lila came over the week after New Year's Day. It was a cold, bitter day, even for the 6th day of 1908 and Jesse had warned Lila to wear heavy clothes and take some extra care in riding over to her mother's. About half way there it began to snow.

Lila was glad she'd ridden their Appaloosa Patches instead of Chief. Jesse had suggested that she take Chief, as he was bigger and younger, but Chief was also ornery, and Lila was afraid that if it snowed he might be spooked. She never forgot the time when she'd given the big horse too much rein and he reached back and nipped at her leg.

The first day the two women went through Ben's closet and most of the drawers in the bureau. Lenora mentioned twice that the snow was really piling up and by nightfall there was six to seven inches accumulated and the snow was still coming down. The women weren't too worried, though, this was part of life on the prairie. Lila even reminded her mother of the time when she was helping Mrs. Osgood with school and they were snowed in nearly four days in the small county schoolhouse.

One look out the bedroom window in the morning told Lila that history might be repeating itself. The snow was at least a foot deep and several feet higher where it drifted. She didn't know whether her mother was up, but then heard noise coming from Lenora's bedroom.

"Mom, what are you doing? It's barely sunup," said Lila, stepping into her mom's room.

"I know, but we need to finish and this keeps my mind off of other things."

"We've got plenty of time, Mom. Have you looked outside?"

"Yes, I have. All right, I'll stop for now. I am a bit hungry. What do you want for breakfast?"

After a hearty breakfast of bacon and eggs, they spent the next several hours sorting Ben's clothes.

"Mom, how about the old trunk as a place to put Dad's things?"

"Yes, I suppose that's as good a spot as any. I think I'll give most of his clothes to the church, but what I keep can be stored in the trunk. It seems fitting. Do you know Lila, that that old trunk has gone from London to Bath England, to New York, then Alton, then Lead and finally here to Ash Creek?"

"I remember you and Dad arguing over whether to leave it in Alton, Mom."

Tears began to well up in Lenora's eyes. "You know, let's just wait until after dinner to do the attic."

"That's fine, Mom. But, why don't you tell me which pile of things goes upstairs and then, while you're getting us something to eat, I'll get started."

The attic was difficult to access. The door to the stairs was in the small bedroom, and after negotiating the narrow stairs, it was necessary to lift a door in the ceiling to enter. Lila hadn't been in the attic in years, but remembered helping her mother carry things up when her parents bought the house from the Jensen family. She especially remembered what a difficult time Jesse and her dad had getting the steamer trunk up the steep incline.

Winsford, England - August 1907

The letter from Martha arrived at the Winsford Post Office in the morning and was delivered to the Franklins later that day. Martha and Lenora's parents moved to the country the previous year after selling the business in Chester.

"It's a letter from Martha, dear," said Clarence.

Clarence and Bertha Franklin had fared well over the past thirty years. The income from selling the fabric shop allowed them to buy a comfortable home on a small acreage just outside of Winsford. They had not seen their daughters since they went to America, but Martha and Lenora wrote often. When they could afford it, they sent photographs of the children and more recently, grandchildren. The Franklins never fully understood their youngest daughter's admonition to keep secret her marriage to Ben Duncan, and told only their closest friends of Lenora's life in America. Martha, too, had asked them to respect her sister's wishes, and like Lenora, had never explained the reasons, only to say that Ben's past was best left unexplored.

"Well, open it Clarence," said Bertha.

"All right Bertha, let me get my glasses."

Clarence opened the envelope and read the letter aloud.

"My dear parents,"

"Sad to say I am writing to tell you of Lenora's husband Ben's passing. I am sure she will write you separately with details. It was a tragic accident. The funeral is tomorrow. All else is fine and we are all praying for Lenora's peace of mind and strength in her time of sorrow."

"Your loving daughter, Martha."

London – 1907

Oren Eflow came into the office only on rare occasions and today was one of those. He was celebrating his 85th birthday and his son, Wendell was taking him to his club. Oren still had an office at the end of the hallway and once in a while surprised the staff by being there before they arrived. Oren always felt that the work day should start at 7 a.m. Such was the case today.

Wendell found him sitting in his favorite red leather chair, reading the letter and card that had arrived yesterday from Angus and Heather.

"Oh, I see you found the letter," said Wendell.

"Yes, and there're pictures of Robert and Scott too."

"See Dad, I told you yesterday that they wouldn't forget."

"America seems so far away. I wish they were closer," said Oren.

After years of working with the Duncombe family in their effort to find William, Oren's firm was put on retainer by Duncombe Shipping to do general investigative work and provide security at their yards. By 1893, Duncombe's New York office and shipyard required full time security and Oren agreed to open up a branch in New York in 1894. Wendell was needed to head the main office in London, so Oren asked his son-in-law, Angus Tetherton, to move to New York and open the office.

Oren's agency had assisted the Duncombes once before in New York, but that time Oren had gone. He'd been much younger then. It had been his idea to request the logs and passenger list from the *S S Blackadder*. The owners of the *Blackadder*, John Willis & Son, had been most cooperative and granted the request. When he saw the entry about the marriage of Ben Duncan to Lenora Franklin, it confirmed to him what he'd already guessed. Ben Duncan was William Duncombe. But that was as far as it went.

The lead dried up in New York. He inquired with immigration, but got nowhere. He checked with various housing authorities, and nothing. It was as if Ben and Lenora never existed. Once, when inquiring on the docks about Ben Duncan, he was roughed up by a couple of goons and told to mind his own business. He later learned the toughs were from Tammany Hall. Returning to England, he reported his failed effort to James Duncombe. That had been almost thirty-five years ago.

Winsford, England – October 1907

Clarence opened the letter from Lenora and read aloud.

"Dear Mother and Father,"

"As Martha has told you, Ben was killed in a thrasher accident last month. I am trying to get along as best I can. The children are helping and Lila and Martha, especially, have given me comfort. Many years ago I asked you not to reveal my marriage to Ben and our leaving to live in America. Now I can tell you the reason. Ben's real name was William Duncombe. My cousin, your nephew, Edward Keith and William got into a business venture which failed and William was blamed. His debts were substantial and he likely would have gone to prison. To this day I believe that Edward was at fault and perhaps even took the missing funds. William just couldn't face his family. I decided to go with him, as I loved him very much. The rest you know, except for my own personal reason for not seeing you before we left."

"I was pregnant and afraid of your rejection, or worse yet, your disappointment. William wanted me to tell you, but I just couldn't face you. William and I got married on the ship and our wonderful son, Willard, was born in America. Ben (William), never wrote to his family after we left, which is sad. When I have time, I may try and locate one of his brothers or sister and write them. I've missed you both so much over the years. I love you. Write soon."

"Your daughter, Lenora"

Bertha was in tears by the time Clarence finished, and he too could not hold back his emotions.

"All those years," he said, wiping his own eyes.

"I'm glad we never gave that Mr. Eflow either of the girls' addresses. It's best that we kept that to ourselves, especially in light of this," Bertha said.

"I think we should write him now, though, don't you think?" said Clarence.

"Yes, I can't see any harm in that, and I have felt very guilty that we weren't up front with him. No harm now, and if he's still alive, he may be able to help Lenora contact Ben's family."

London – October 1907

Oren lived in the Alpinam Apartments, near Collingwood House, on Cavendish Street. He could enter from the ground floor and the three rooms were adequate for his needs. His wife, Cynthia had passed on the previous year.

His children, especially his daughter when she visited from America, were constantly after him to move into a health facility, but he refused. She told Wendell that a better-managed diet would help their father's weight problem. Oren, however, ignored his daughter's pleadings. He was perfectly happy. He had his prize-winning rose garden, a reliable housekeeper, and a visiting nurse once a week. That was enough for him.

Wendell knocked twice, but got no answer. He was getting concerned, when the door opened. There stood his father, attired in his nightclothes, holding a flickering candle.

"Do you know what time it is, Wendell?" he said.

"Yes, Father, eight-fifteen. I was worried when I got no answer."

"I'm not in my dotage yet! You should know by now that at eight I have finished my evening meal, had my bath and retired for the day."

"I know, Father," he said, impatiently, "but we received a registered letter today from a Clarence Franklin in Winsford, and I thought you should see it. Sorry I couldn't get here earlier."

"A letter from Clarence Franklin. That certainly brings back memories. All right, come in. Let's see the letter."

Chapter Ten

Lenora added a few more slices of ham to the soup and put another piece of wood in the stove. She could hear Lila moving around in the attic. She had just carried up the last load of clothes.

"Lila," she hollered, "the soup's just about done, come down and have some." Not getting any response, she left the kitchen and walked into the bedroom.

"Lila," she shouted again.

"Yes, I'll be right there, I'm just about finished," Lila said.

Several minutes passed before Lenora heard Lila coming down the stairs. She was just finishing dishing up the soup when she sensed Lila standing behind her.

"Mama, who is William Duncombe?"

Lenora almost dropped one of the bowls. "What did you say?"

"I said, who is William Duncombe? I found these letters and a telegram stuck in the lining of one of the pockets in the steamer trunk. They're all addressed to William Duncombe."

Lenora set the bowls down and extended her hand. "Let me see." Her hand shook as she took them and slowly sat down.

There were three letters and a telegram all addressed to William Duncombe at his Edgar Street flat in Bath. One of the letters caught her attention right away. It had six penny postage stamps, and on the rear, had the embossed monogram of Malcolm Jones, Barrister. This letter had a circular date stamp on the back indicating it had been sent from London on 10 October 1871. *Just a few days before they sailed*, she thought.

"Well, Mama, did you and father know this Mr. Duncombe?" Lenora had forgotten, momentarily, about Lila and her question.

"Yes, I guess you could say that, dear."

Lenora thought about all the years gone by and how many times she and her husband had debated over telling the children of the past. The children always knew about her parents in Chester and they'd never lied about the fact that they left England because of financial problems. However, concerning their father, they had been told that his parents were dead and that there were no siblings. Ben had insisted upon this. He'd only gotten along with his brothers James and Terrance and, although he had a good relationship with his father, he couldn't face the knowledge that his financial blunder would devastate his father. As the years passed, Ben assumed that his father was dead, but he never tried to contact any of his siblings.

Lila was watching her mother and could see that she was hesitating. "Mama," she said again.

"William Duncombe was your father."

"What? Mama!"

"Yes, that was his name before we came to America. Sit down, dear. I guess it's time you knew the story. We should have told you years ago."

London – October 1907

Oren adjusted his glasses and turned the wick up on the lamp. He read slowly and when he finished he was smiling.

"I'm glad I've lived long enough to learn the answer to a mystery that's been unsolved for almost thirty-five years."

"What's that, Father?"

"The Duncombe family mystery. You remember, don't you? I guess you were quite young when it all started, but I've told you about it several times. The youngest Duncombe, William, disappeared in 1871."

"I remember, but didn't you figure out that he had sailed for America under an assumed name and married someone from Chester on the voyage?"

"Yes, but the trail disappeared in New York. I wrote the Franklins, they are the parents of the woman he married, and told them, but I never heard back from them."

"Wasn't there also some kind of riddle or puzzle that involved the Duncombe inheritance?"

"Yes, there was. It was very strange. The senior Duncombe wrote each of the five children a letter and contained within the letter was a puzzle to the location of a sizeable sum of money. As I understood it, and they never really told me the finer details, all five letters needed to be put together to find the solution."

"So what happened when they couldn't locate the son?"

"Here again, I wasn't privy to all of it, but I understand that, other than the hidden funds, the balance of the estate ended up being divided among the surviving four."

"So, they must have declared him legally dead after so many years?"

"Yes," answered Oren.

"But the hidden funds, wouldn't Mr. Duncombe have provided for the possibility of one of the children not being found, or worse, being deceased?" Wendell said.

"Once again, I'm somewhat faint on this. I'm repeating myself, but remember, it <u>was</u> years ago. James Duncombe told me that there was a back up plan left with Duncombe's barrister. Supposedly after so much time expired and the children had not found the hidden funds, the barrister was to open sealed documents that would reveal the location."

"So, he'd divide it up among the children then?"

"No, it would go to charity."

"Good god, what a weird legacy," said Wendell. "Then it all went to charity?"

"No. Ironically there was a fire in '72 that destroyed the barrister's office, killed him and his assistant."

"And the documents, I assume they were lost too?"

"Yes," said Oren.

"Then the treasure trove may still be hidden," said Wendell.

Oren laid the letter down. "I assume so. I understand the four children tried to solve the puzzle without success. Even after my initial help, I was never entirely informed, even though we have continued to be involved with the Duncombe family in our business."

"Are they all alive?"

"The ones here in England are, but this letter from the Franklins tells of the death of William in America. It appears that the Franklins knew of their daughter's location, but were never made privy to the fact that she was married to William Duncombe. I don't understand why they didn't because I told them what I'd learned."

"Maybe they never got your letter," said Wendell.

"Maybe not. That would explain it."

"What other details are in the letter?"

"Here, see for yourself," said Oren.

Wendell took the letter from his father and held it near the lamp.

"So, he's been in America all this time. I gather from this that his wife Lenora never told the Franklins."

"She appears to have told them about her husband's reasons for leaving, but not that he was William Duncombe," said Oren.

"It says in this letter that she may try to contact the Duncombe family. Won't they be surprised." Wendell paused for a minute. "Say, Father, I wonder what happened to the missing letter?"

"Who knows, but you'd think that if they found it, they would have contacted someone in the family." Oren walked across the room and put his arm around his son.

"Thanks for bringing this. Sorry I barked at you. Let me think about it, but maybe we should contact the Duncombes ourselves. For now, I'm tired and need to get to bed. I'll stop by the office in the morning."

Terrance Duncombe was nearing age sixty-seven and was reluctantly turning over the reins of Pulteney Publishing to his partner and long time friend, Maxwell Bennington. There had been many times in the past when he'd wished they'd not bought the business from the Pulteneys. Those first years were the roughest. Trying to run the business, while at the same time continuing to send money to Anne Spencer, pay blackmail to Edward Keith and keep it all quiet from Evelyn.

If it hadn't been for the inheritance, he could never have managed. Of course, if they'd located the treasure his father had hidden, that would have helped tremendously. But that never happened. The payments to Anne stopped seventeen years ago when Henry reached age twenty-one and joined the Dragoon Guards.

The meetings with Edward Keith in London came to a halt in 1893. How Keith originally found out about his relationship with Anne, he never knew, but he couldn't risk Evelyn knowing and being ostracized by the family. Keith always wrote and confirmed their annual meeting place in London, and Terrance dutifully met him with the money. Then, suddenly it was over. Why, he never knew. He never got a letter in 1893 and never heard from Keith again.

Although his affair with Anne Spencer ended many years ago, Terrance saw her at Henry's university graduation and then once again in 1899 when Henry came home from the Boer War. His injuries had been extensive and his career in the army was at an end. That was when Anne had suggested that he hire Henry. At first he was averse to the idea, especially since Stephen worked at the firm, but Anne kept pushing him and finally he agreed. He had one condition which was, that Henry not reveal their relationship.

Henry turned out to be a good employee and, despite his worry about someone in Bath discovering that Henry was his son, Terrance came to enjoy knowing him. Two potentially dangerous situations did emerge, however.

First was when Henry went to work in Stephen's Pressroom Department. Maybe it was only noticeable to Terrance, but when the two of them stood together, there was a strong resemblance. Terrance's fears were for naught. Henry and Stephen became friends at work and as far as Terrance knew, no one ever guessed they were half-brothers.

The second problem situation arose when Olivia Kirkland came to work at the firm during the summer of 1900. They'd been looking for a factory nurse and his sister Mary suggested her daughter Olivia, who was working at a hospital in Birmingham. She was still unmarried at thirty-two. Mary told Terrance of one particular relationship, but Terrance gathered that she was devoted to her job and not much else. Terrance hadn't seen her in several years, but remembered her as somewhat plain and that she had unfortunately inherited the Duncombe propensity for being stout.

Henry's occasional bouts with malaria required doses of quinine and the first week that Olivia came to work, Henry had an attack. For Henry it was love at first sight. Olivia, too, was immediately attracted to Henry, who in spite of his limp and scarred face, was a very good-looking man.

By the time Terrance heard of the budding romance, Henry and Olivia met twice for lunch and, according to Stephen, they'd had more than one night out at the local dance hall. For awhile he said nothing, which turned out to be a mistake. Finally, he called Henry into his office after work. He recalled the conversation.

"Henry, thanks for staying late."

"Sure, is there a problem?"

"Actually, there is, but not between you and I or concerning your work, which according to Stephen, is just fine, by the way" said Terrance.

"What then, is mother ill?"

"No. What we need to talk about is your relationship with Olivia Kirkland."

Terrance could see Henry tensing up. "My relationship, as you call it, with Olivia, is none of your business. Why should you care? We don't do anything to interfere with our work."

Henry rose and turned to leave.

"She's your cousin, Henry." *How odd that Olivia didn't tell Henry she was my niece,* he thought.

"What!" He whirled around. Terrance continued, now fully aware by Henry's reaction that he didn't have prior knowledge.

"Yes, she's my sister Mary's daughter. I know we haven't talked that much about my family since you came here to work, but ----." Henry interrupted.

"That was your idea, don't put that burden on me – Father!" Henry's face telegraphed his odious feelings.

"Don't raise your voice, young man. I'm warning you for your own good. For one thing, Tyler Kirkland, Mary's husband knew of my relationship with your mother and I know Mary did too." Henry started to say something, but Terrance raised his hand and continued.

"Secondly, she's your blood relation."

Henry's shoulders went slack. "But, we're in love," he said.

"Hopefully you've been prudent in your relationship," Terrance said.

Terrance could tell by the look on Henry's face that he had not.

"This has got to stop, now," Terrance said. "I will not have it! If I have to tell her, I will!"

Henry started to move toward his father in a threatening manner, but then stopped. "All right."

Henry left the office and to this day, Terrance never knew what happened, but Olivia resigned her position the next month. His relationship with Henry was never the same.

Terrance did learn through Stephen that Henry was still involved with Olivia and traveled to Birmingham to see her after she moved back, but he never brought the subject up to his son Henry again.

James Duncombe met Madeline Fortier at the reception for Edward Elgar, following the London performance of his overture, *Froissart*. Duncombe Shipping had always been a patron of the arts, but James seldom attended any of the social events. In 1890, at fifty-three years, he was still considered one of London's most eligible bachelors, but he resigned himself to being unmarried, despite the efforts of several of his married friends. It was his friends the Fenwicks that insisted he attend the premier of the opera *Froissart*.

Madeline Fortier opened her art gallery in 1889 when she moved from Paris to London. Some said she left France after a failed marriage, but no one knew for sure. What people did know was that she was very wealthy and her gallery catered to the elite of London society. Within a year of her arriving on the London scene, she was invited to all the major social events. Madeline wore the latest Paris fashions and the cut of her gowns left no doubt about the well-rounded figure they covered. Though forty-one, she had the look of a much younger woman and never lacked for a male companion at social events.

As James was soon to discover, Madeline possessed many attributes, including no lack of passion for, or experience in, the art of making love. From first meeting, James was immediately attracted to her and, although Madeline was at the onset just interested in a casual sexual liaison, she gradually fell in love with James. They became the talk of London and were married in June of the following year. The wedding at St. Paul's was the highlight of the season.

Terrance was James' best man and, with the exception of Michael Duncombe, who was in Canada, the rest of the family attended. Madeline's mother from Paris was her daughter's matron of honor.

Giles and Ruth arrived from York the day before the wedding and, though James invited them to stay with him, they got rooms at the Rhodes House Hotel on Sussex Gardens.

Giles had given up his position at the university several years previous. He and Ruth were comfortably retired to the family farm. They rarely saw their children and had few visitors. Michael had a teaching position at Toronto University in Canada, was unmarried and visited home sporadically. Sarah was married to Percy Munroe and they lived in Edinburgh. They had two daughters, Emily and Ilene, who Giles said, for anyone who wanted to hear, were becoming Scot's and forgetting their English heritage.

It didn't used to be so quiet at the farm. For more years than he could remember there was a constant parade of family members searching the house, all the out buildings and looking in every conceivable place for the hidden treasure. Solving the riddle became a full-time job for some and a constant quest for most. They all had agreed that the clues led to York and most likely to the farm. The last several letters seemed to spell out a particular location, *UP FOUR LEFT,* but from where?

Finally, most gave up and admitted that, without the missing letter and envelope, they had little chance. Some, like Mary and Tyler kept coming back every summer, but then, they too eventually stopped searching. Once in a while, as Giles puttered around the old farm, he got an idea, but it always ended up in a wild goose chase.

Now, Giles, like the rest of the family, had surrendered any hope of solving the riddle and finding the treasure left by their father so many years before. He often thought. *Strange that six little red penny postage stamps held the key to so much.*

October - December 1907

The letters from Oren Eflow first reached Terrance and James, then a day later, Mary and Giles. Oren told them of his correspondence from the Franklins and their letter from Lenora Duncan. The four siblings had similar reactions over the news, that William, who had called himself Ben, had been alive, married with three children and living in America. Eflow's letter also said that Lenora might try to contact the family. The question in all their minds was whether she could shed any light on the letter written to her husband. The letter with the envelope that might, after all these years, solve the puzzle. James wondered whether he should contact Lenora directly instead of waiting for her letter, if she wrote at all. She would not know their addresses. Giles had similar thoughts. Eflow included Lenora's address in his letter. James thought, *Ash Creek, South Dakota, sounds like it's in the middle of nowhere.*

By mid-November, when no one in the family had received any correspondence from Lenora, James decided it was time to take some action. But what action? Should he write to her and be very direct about the missing letter? He decided to have Oren's firm make the contact and wrote to his siblings for their advice. They all agreed but Mary, who felt a more personal letter of condolence from the family should be their first step, if they didn't hear from Lenora by the first of December. No letter was received.

At the end of the first week in December, James made an appointment to see Oren and his son, Wendell. The meeting concluded with the decision that Oren would write the letter.

When Oren finished the letter, he stopped by his office so he could review it with his son. Wendell was in early, as he half expected his father. He even had the tea water ready.

"Tea, Father?"

"Yes. Here's the draft of the Duncombe letter." He laid the piece of paper on Wendell's desk.

"Sit down Father. Why don't you read it aloud for me?" Wendell said, handing his father a cup of tea.

Oren nodded, took a seat opposite his son and began.

Dear Mrs. Duncan,

On behalf of the Duncombe family I offer their condolences and prayers on learning of the death of your husband and their brother, William. You can imagine their shock to learn that William, whom you call Ben, was alive all these years and living in America.

William's father died in 1871. His three brothers and sister still reside in England. You may not be aware of the fact that the family paid the debt owed by William, although they suspect that a Mr. Edward Keith may have taken advantage of your husband and been the cause of the failure.

You are also likely unaware of the provisions in the will of William's father. In particular, his plan to unite the family using a rather unique approach that involved a riddle sent to each of the children. To solve the riddle and find a sizeable treasure, all five letters and especially their envelopes, had to be used together. William may or may not have ever received his letter or the telegram sent advising of his father's death.

If you can shed any light on this, the family would be forever grateful and, it is very likely that you will gain financially. Again, our sincere condolences.

Respectfully, Oren Eflow, Eflow & Sons, Investigations.

They sent the letter the week before Christmas.

Birmingham, England – December 1907

When Henry traveled north to meet Olivia, they usually met in Wolverhampton, a small town near Birmingham. Most of the time they stayed at The Wolverhampton Hotel. It was on Lichfield Street, in a quiet section, but within walking distance of several cafés and two theaters. Olivia loved the theater, especially Shakespeare, and when the Drury Lane players were at the Dorridge they always went when Henry was in town. Henry wasn't so keen on Shakespeare, preferring the lighter comedy revues and follies at the Pennington, but nevertheless, always went to please Olivia.

After the nasty encounter with Terrance, Henry decided to tell Olivia the truth. She was as shocked as he had been. They decided to stop seeing each other for a time and then see how they felt, but with them both working at the same place, that didn't last long and they were soon back in each other's arms, their passion greater than before. Then Olivia suddenly had second thoughts, quit her job and returned to Birmingham.

Henry was distraught and his ire toward his father was hard not to show. He came close to barging into his office on more than one occasion. Finally, two months after she left, Olivia wrote to Henry, her words pouring out her love for him. Henry took the train to Birmingham the next day. That was almost six years ago.

Henry had several times thought about quitting his job and moving closer to Birmingham, but in the end, he stayed in Bath and the lovers met as often as they could. Over the Christmas holiday this year they decided it was time to leave England, get married and start a new life in Canada.

They saved enough to buy a passage for two, but not much else. Even though the government paid a portion of Henry's medical bills, his share of the costs of the monthly treatment for his malaria-damaged kidneys ate up what little reserve they had. One doctor told Henry that his disease likely made him infertile, but he continued to use protection. He and Olivia decided that they should never chance having children.

The plan was to leave in May. Henry hoped they would soon have more money to start their new life, and once in Canada, be able to pay for his mother's passage. More and more he came to agree with his mother's constant reminder that he'd been cheated of his inheritance.

His mother still lived in London in a small flat in Kensington. She had never married, and as far as he knew, had never had a long-term relationship since he was a boy. He figured her forward nature and nonconformity eventually scared the men away.

Of course, there was his father, who visited often in the early years, and then the man that lived with them for a year or so. He was told to call him Uncle Edward.

He corresponded with Edward several times a year and just recently wrote him at his new address in Toronto. It was from his "uncle" that he got the idea of moving to Canada.

Chapter Eleven

The only sound in the room was the noise of the wind blowing on the shutters as the snowstorm raged on.

"And no one knew?" Lila said.

"Only Martha and Mickey," Lenora answered.

"Not Grandma and Grandpa Franklin?"

"No, they only knew that your father and I left England under suspicious circumstances, but never knew his real name was William Duncombe."

Lila started to say something, but Lenora raised her hand and continued. "I wrote to them in October. So they know now."

"How about the Duncombe family?" Lila asked.

"No. I thought about it, but haven't as yet. Actually, I don't really know if any of his brothers or sister are alive and I wouldn't know where to start."

"How many brothers did he have?"

"Three brothers and one sister," said Lenora.

"Do you want to open the letters and the telegram, or shall I?" Lila said.

"You do it, dear, I just can't."

Lila first opened the telegram and read aloud the message sent from Malcolm Jones that told of the death of Giles Duncombe and requesting William's presence at the funeral. The first two letters were from a Stanton Beasly of Barclays Bank in Chester England.

"This Mr. Beasly sounds very upset, especially in the second letter," said Lila.

"Yes, I suspect he was. What puzzles me is how these letters ended up in the trunk. Look, they're dated several days before William left his flat and look at the envelopes, they've been opened, but William never mentioned them?"

"The telegram hasn't been opened and this other letter still has an unbroken seal," Lila said.

"Well, let's see what that one says. Strange that the envelope has six stamps. Open it up, Lila, and I'll read this one."

Lenora finished and handed the letter to Lila. As she did, she reached across and took the envelope. Other than the six stamps, she didn't see anything particularly odd about it, but the letter had been clear, *Save the envelopes* ---. And a treasure! She'd really never speculated about any inheritance up till now. *Wouldn't that be something*, she thought.

Lila finished the letter and then reached for the envelope. "How very strange. I mean the whole thing. Mother, you could be rich!"

"I doubt it, dear. After all these years, I'm sure there's really nothing to it. I would guess they decided long ago that your father was dead. Besides, it all sounds like a pipe dream to me anyway. Although your father used to tell me about the treasure hunts the family had in York and the riddles they had to solve to find hidden treasure."

"What do you think we should do now?"

"Nothing, really. I think we'd best let the past alone."

"But Mother, I probably have all sorts of relatives and just think, if you got some money you could afford to paint the house like you and Father wanted to do for years."

Lenora laughed. "You just want to change the color, I know. Your Father didn't like the stucco painted red either, but I love it!"

Their laughter broke the tension and Lenora took the letter and envelope and laid them on the kitchen counter. "I think that's enough for now. As I said, better to let sleeping dogs lie."

"Oh Mother, you always say that. At least we need to tell Willard and Chester and the other family members," Lila said.

"Yes, at least Willard and Chester," she said.

Lila knew from past experience that the conversation was over. She put away the soup bowls and returned to the attic to finish packing the trunk. As she worked, her thoughts continued to be on what she had just learned. *Won't Jesse be surprised*, she thought. She hoped the snow would abate soon. She could hardly wait to get home and tell him the news.

The snow did let up long enough for Lila to ride home, and the next morning it started again and by noon, Lenora could tell that they were really in for it. She was well provisioned and she'd been through hard winters before. She knew Jesse and Lila would help with the cattle if it got too bad.

Days turned into weeks and the snowfall kept up until Lenora could barely see out her windows. She would learn later that they had over sixty-three inches between January the 8th and February 17, a record for Stanley County. When it finally stopped, it took Jesse and his brother Howard another week just to clear a path so they could reach the main road to town.

Jesse told Lenora that he was going into Philip for spring supplies and to get the mail on Tuesday and suggested she go with him. Women seldom made the trip to town and never alone. She readily agreed and was ready to go when he pulled up to the house with Prince hitched to the wagon.

The nearest post office to Ash Creek was in Philip and the country people picked up the mail on their infrequent trips to town. They were supposed to get a post office in Hilland this year. The Campbell family would run it and the news last year was that they would also open a general store.

Lenora usually did her grocery shopping first at Clement's Market, picked up her millinery needs, and then stopped by the post office on Main Street. Jesse made the trip to Philip as often as he could to visit with his folks who had moved in from the country two years before. On this trip, they would stay overnight at the Mason's, as the trip was too long for one day, especially this winter.

There was only one other wagon at Clement's, so Jesse had plenty of room to tie Prince to the rail.

"I'll check on my folks first, Lenora, and meet you back here."

The Clement's son Jim helped load Lenora's supplies in the wagon and as Jesse had not returned, she decided to walk down to the post office, not needing anything else this trip.

"Jimmy, you tell Jesse that I've gone to the post office and I'll meet him back here." With that she headed down Main Street.

Lenora never liked Mrs. Spurwell. She was the nosiest person in Philip and always acted like she was doing you a favor when she handed you your mail. Martha was convinced that Betsy Spurwell somehow peeked inside all the letters because she knew everything that was going on in town and in Stanley County, for that matter.

"Got plenty of mail for you Lenora, including one registered letter from London, England, no less." Betsy said it loud enough for anyone else in the post office to hear, and Lenora guessed even the people next door at Sandal's Hardware knew she had a letter from England.

"Thank you, Betsy," Lenora said, quietly. She took the letter and turned to leave.

"You have to sign for it," she said with practiced authority.

"I suppose so," said Lenora.

Betsy produced an official looking form and Lenora signed her name. "Must be important, coming all the way from London, and registered mail, too," said Betsy.

"Must be," said Lenora, who gave a slight smile and left the Post Office. *Busybody*, she thought.

When she got back to Clement's, Jesse was still loading his supplies.

"How are your folks, Jesse?"

"Just fine. They're looking forward to seeing you. Mom's cooking fried chicken for us. She said supper's at five."

Lenora hadn't eaten for a while and she was dying to open and read the special letter. *Think I'll have a cup of tea and a piece of pie, and maybe just read this letter before going over to Leroy and Millie's.* Lenora turned to Jesse.

"That sound's fine, I'm going to go down to the diner for some tea while you finish here. Take your time."

She said hello to Mrs. Olsen and her young son as she passed them. *Just think*, she thought, *it wasn't that many years ago that Willard was his age and Ben and I were living in Alton.*

The diner was empty except for old Mr. Bailey and George Ferguson sitting at the counter, so Lenora had her pick of the four booths.

When Esther came out from the kitchen, she asked Lenora what she wanted.

"What kind of pie?"

"Apple and Peach, today."

"Apple will be fine, and I'll have some tea," said Lenora.

"Want a scoop of ice cream on the pie?"

"No, thanks." She noticed George looking at her.

"Hello, George. In town for supplies?" She already knew the answer, because for most of the farmers, the occasional trips to Philip were for that very reason.

"Yes and to get the mail and to get Flaxey shoed," he said.

"How's Laura?" Lenora asked.

"She's fine thanks. Glad winter's finally over," he said. "How you getting along?"

"Fine, thanks. I came into town with Jesse."

George nodded and took a drink from his coffee, just as Esther came around the counter with Lenora's pie and the coffeepot.

"More coffee, George?" She refreshed his cup and walked to Lenora's booth.

"Here's the pie. I'll be back with your tea," she said.

Lenora waited until she'd been served the tea and then opened the envelope. Inside was another envelope with the London address of Eflow Investigations, a new US five dollar bill and a letter from Oren Eflow. She started reading.

She heard someone walking toward her and looked up. "Something wrong with the pie?" Esther asked.

Lenora realized she hadn't had a bite. "No, sorry."

She made a show at eating while she continued reading. Esther retreated back to the counter and busied herself filling Mr. Bailey's coffee cup. Lenora could tell she was dying to see what she was doing. Lenora looked at the letter again and her only thought was maybe Lila was right, the old house may get painted after all. *Still red, though*, she thought.

She chuckled, a bit too loud.

"You say something, Lenora?" asked George.

"No. Just amused at something I'm reading."

George rose from the counter and went to the cash register. As he did, he looked back toward Lenora. "Be sure and let us know if we can help in any way," he said.

"I will, George, and thanks. Say hello to Laura for me."

Lenora finished her pie and tea and left twenty-five cents on the table. *Time to find Jesse*, she thought.

The sky was beginning to darken and she saw a flash of lightening in the west. The rural roads were bad enough with all the snow and it would be really a mess if they got rained on to boot. Lenora was glad they weren't going to try and get home today. More than once, they had gotten stuck in the mud. *They.* It was still hard to get used to not thinking in the plural after thirty-five years.

It started to pour just as Lenora got back to Clement's. Jesse got Prince unhitched and they quickly headed for the Masons. Then, just as fast as the rain had started, it stopped. *Strange for this time of year*, she thought, *more like a summerstorm.*

The first morning after getting home, Lenora was still uncertain about how to respond to the letter. She thought about riding over to see Lila after she got back, but remembered Jesse told her that Lila and Ginnie Mitchell from Marietta were going to try and get out an issue of the Ash Creek Pilot. The last printing of the local newspaper had been just before Christmas.

She decided instead to go see Martha.

It was just after sunrise when she left for Martha's. The snow was melting fast, but there was still a chill in the air and she'd bundled up for the ride.

Oblivious to the cold, Martha was sitting on the porch, wrapped up in a quilt reading her Bible when Lenora rode up.

"Morning, Lenora. What brings you over so early this morning?"

"Got a letter from England, that concerns Ben and his family," she said.

"I heard you got a registered letter," Martha said.

"Should have figured that Betsy would spread the news." She dismounted and unbuckled Prince's saddle cinch.

Martha removed the quilt and set her Bible aside. "Just leave his saddle on for now and put him in the corral, and come on in, I'll make some coffee."

Before showing Martha the letter from Oren Eflow, she told her of Lila's discovery in the old steamer trunk and handed her the telegram and letter she'd brought along.

"So Lila knows?"

"Yes and I think it was about time," said Lenora.

"I assume the letter you got has something to do with this?" She handed her sister the new letter.

As they drank their coffee, Martha read the letter from Oren Eflow. "Wow. What a surprise, Lenora, it sounds like you're going to be rich. What a coincidence that you just found the letter to William."

"Actually, before Lila left last month, I had just about decided to forget the whole thing. It was so long ago and I doubt there's really any treasure left to be found." She hesitated. "Now I'm not sure what to do. Plus, with the snow and all, it's been almost two months since this letter arrived. They probably wonder why I haven't answered."

"Of course, they don't know you found the letter and the

telegram in the trunk," said Martha.

"No, they don't."

"If it were up to me, I'd send a telegram to this Mr. Eflow."

"But the telegraph lines don't come to Philip."

"You'd have to go to Fort Pierre or Deadwood and right now, that's not possible," said Martha.

"Maybe once the roads are better I can have someone send a telegram for me from Fort Pierre," Lenora said.

"The way it looks right now, that may be awhile," Martha said.

The two sisters spent the rest of the day talking about the letter and how Lenora should respond. The conversation eventually turned to their early days in New York and how ironical it was that the letters and telegram were in the old trunk that Mickey and William had struggled to get into their room.

"It seems so long ago," said Lenora.

"Yes, it does. Speaking of 'long ago,' I read in the *Black Hills Weekly Journal* that President Roosevelt announced he won't run for re-election next year."

"Where did you see a newspaper?"

"Betsy Spurwell had one at the Post Office. Anyway, I wonder whether he'll come back to the Dakotas?"

"You continue to write to him once in a while, don't you?"

"Yes," answered Martha. "Just think, he has six children of his own now. By the way, in his last letter he said to say hello to you and Ben."

"Ben and I. Oh, Martha, I miss him so."

"I know Lenora, and I think contacting Mr. Eflow would be something that Ben would have wanted."

"You're right, of course. When the roads clear, I'll do it."

London, England - March 2, 1908

The telegram arrived at Eflow Investigations on March 2nd. After reading it, Wendell left the office for his father's rooms. Wendell couldn't believe it. After all this time. He knew his father had given up hope of ever hearing from Lenora Duncan and just a week ago, he himself, had contacted James Duncombe with the bad news. He assumed that by now, all the Duncombes had resigned themselves to the fact that they would never have the missing piece of the puzzle. *"It'll go down as the penny red enigma"* his father had been saying.

Oren was home and just finishing reading *The Times*. Without any prelude, Wendell handed him the telegram and took a seat.

"So, she found the letter. Incredible! Her message still leaves a lot of unanswered questions," Oren said, as he handed the telegram back to Wendell.

"At least we know she has it, and I gather she didn't get your letter until recently. That's odd, don't you think?"

"No, not really. She likely lives in a rural area and I read recently that parts of the Dakotas in America were isolated for weeks because of record snowfalls. Either way, she has it now."

"But she doesn't say much beyond that. Is she going to send it to us, or what?"

Oren reached for his pipe and said nothing as he added tobacco from the box on the mantel. In deep thought, he lit the pipe and sat back down.

"I have an idea," he said. "We should send Angus to South Dakota."

"Shouldn't we let the Duncombes know?"

"Well yes. They need to be told that we've heard from Mrs. Duncan and that she has the letter and then I think they will agree that, at this point, we need to take a direct approach. The last thing we want to happen is for Mrs. Duncan to mail the letter and have it get lost."

"She doesn't say anything about sending it," Wendell said.

"I know, but she might. Even worse, she may try to do some puzzle solving on her own and destroy the stamps in the process," Oren said.

"Fine, I'll go see James Duncombe today and, if he thinks it's all right, I'll telegraph Terrance, Giles and Mary Kirkland."

"He may want to do that himself, Wendell. The main thing is to get him to see the merit in personally contacting Mrs. Duncan in America, and as soon as possible."

James readily agreed on the plan to have Oren's son-in-law in America contact Lenora Duncan. He also accepted Wendell's offer to advise the other family members that Oren had heard from Lenora, that she had the missing letter and that Eflow Investigations' branch in the United States would meet with Lenora Duncan.

The next day, Wendell sent a telegram to his brother-in-law Angus Tetherton, in New York. He also sent a registered letter to Lenora Duncan in South Dakota.

Family on the South Dakota Prairie – 1908

Chapter Twelve

"Ever been in South Dakota before?"

"No. Actually, Pastor, until this trip I'd never been west of Pittsburgh."

"Please call me Paul," he said.

They'd been traveling the same road for hours and mostly talked about New York City, England, and Angus' train trip. Angus did learn that Paul Blanton was a widower and lived in Powell, but his occasional queries about the Duncans revealed little that he didn't already know. *For a preacher*, Angus thought, *he doesn't say much*.

Angus wasn't really sure it was the same road. *There are certainly no street signs out here*, he'd said to himself on more than one occasion. With no landmarks, and no perceptible change in elevation, he lost all perspective. He knew their general direction was north, because the sun was on his left.

The wheel ruts left by others before them had hardened in the sun and Blanton's horse, Old Blue, was having a tough time pulling the two-seat buckboard and extra weight. The potholes were also beginning to take a heavy toll on Angus' rear end.

"Starting to get dark, we'd better look for a spot to camp for the night," said Blanton.

Angus had arrived in Philip on Thursday and after talking to the stationmaster and a man at the General store, he began to realize that getting to Ash Creek and the Duncan place was going to be no easy task. The man at the livery took one look at his Houndstooth vest and high button shoes, and laughed aloud when Angus asked about renting a buggy to go to Lenora's.

"It's almost forty miles, you know," he said, choking off another laugh. "You sound like you're from Canada."

"No, New York," said Angus.

"Well you sure sound like one of them," he said.

"I used to live in England," said Angus, now more frustrated with his predicament. *Let's hope all the locals aren't like this fellow,* he thought. He thanked the man at the livery, without sounding too sarcastic, and walked back down Main Street to where he'd earlier seen a hotel.

It was just after five when he checked into the Seneshal Hotel. It was at supper that he got a break. Sitting at the table next to him was Pastor Paul Blanton. Blanton was talking to his dinner companion about his trip the next day to Ash Creek. Listening in, Angus, learned that Blanton usually left on Friday, stopped enroute and arrived at Ash Creek early Saturday. When Blanton and his guest finished, Angus rose and introduced himself. Leaving out a few details, he explained his need to see Lenora Duncan and asked if he could accompany Blanton on his trip to Ash Creek.

And now, here he was, he thought. *It was getting dark.*

"Normally, I stay with the Keysers, but they're in Pierre."

"How often do you make this trip?"

"This time of year, I'm lucky if I get out here once a month," he said. "Normally, once every other week."

"Here's a good place to pull off." Blanton said. "My sixty year old bones are ready for a good rest."

Paul Blanton was well liked by all the parishioners he served in Stanley County. He and his wife, Emma, had moved from Kirley to Midland in 1896. It was their sixth church since he completed seminary in Minnesota, and at age forty-nine, he hoped they could serve out his ministry in Midland, and then return to their hometown of Pierre. They had no children. Both wanted a family, but after three miscarriages, the doctors had warned them about the danger to Emma if they tried again.

They'd been in Midland for six years when an outbreak of smallpox hit western South Dakota. Paul caught the disease, but recovered. Emma did not, and at fifty-five he found himself a widower and alone.

Paul was a gentle man with a broad smile and medium stature. Those that assumed gentleness meant weakness soon learned that years of working in the fields and on the railroad in his youth, had given him the strength of a blacksmith. More than once he helped out with branding and was always ready to pitch in at a barn raising. He always said, "he was just doing the Lord's work."

After a year in Midland without Emma, he knew he had to leave. The memories were just too painful. When he heard that Pastor Sid Thurston was retiring in Powell, he applied for, and got the job. None of the congregations in Powell, Philip, Ash Creek, Hilland or Marietta could afford to support a full time pastor, so like Pastor Thurston, he would travel the circuit and divide his time among the five churches.

In 1903 he moved into the small parsonage in Powell and began his ministry in rural Stanley County. The first friends he made were Ben and Lenora Duncan.

When Angus Tetherton approached him at dinner, Paul had at first been reluctant to say yes to Tetherton's request. The man looked like one of those eastern dandies and he couldn't believe that Lenora Duncan would have any reason to see him. However, after he talked to him for a while, he consented. He felt deep down that Tetherton had a broader agenda than he let on. Either way, he'd be with him when they got to the Duncan place, so he could make sure everything was on the up and up.

Since Ben's death he'd visited several times with Lenora and her family and recently sat with her at a box social in Ash Creek. He had to admit to himself that he was taking a bit more than a pastor's interest in her.

He also had to confess that having a chance to visit her home influenced his decision to take Angus Tetherton with him to Ash Creek. Tetherton sure had plied him for information about the Duncans, but he had steered the questioning away from that subject by asking about New York and England.

Like just about everyone that picked up their mail in Powell or Philip, Blanton had heard about the registered letter Lenora received and was curious to know how his passenger fit into the picture. That was Lenora's business though, and for now he'd just focus on getting them to Ash Creek.

He glanced at his passenger as he jumped down from the buckboard. Although not overly masculine looking, especially in his eastern attire, Tetherton appeared to be in fit shape. *He's probably ten years younger than I am*, thought Blanton. *At least his hair is not getting gray like mine.*

The sound of the horse whinnying woke Angus. He was very cold and wet. It had rained during the night. *Great!,* he thought, *that's all we need to make the road even worse.*

Blanton was already up and giving the horse the hay that he'd used under his blanket during the night, so it was nice and dry. After drinking some water and eating some of the leftover beans and bread from their meal last night, they hitched up Old Blue and headed out. *Cold beans for breakfast! So this is country living,* thought Angus.

There was no sign indicating they were nearing Ash Creek, but Angus spotted a few buildings ahead.

"Looks a little smaller than I had envisioned," he said.

"Oh, this isn't Ash Creek, this is Hilland. We still have a ways to go, about seven miles, but we'll stop here long enough to dry off and get warm and have a cup of coffee."

The road from Hilland wasn't much different and if anything, it was a lot bumpier.

"Will you take me out to the Duncans after we get there?"

"Oh sure. I'll stop at the church first, but I should have you there by dusk," Blanton answered.

When they left Ash Creek the road leveled off and a house and barn came into view. No other buildings were visible as he scanned the horizon, so Angus assumed it must be the Duncan place.

The house was brick red except for the white window and door trim. A windbreak of several elm and cottonwood trees, most looking half-dead, stood just north of the house.

Blanton slowed for a curve, and then for a narrow wooden bridge spanning an overflowing creek. Here the road was overgrown with weeds, except for two wheel ruts. There were several horses in the corral and a large wagon was near the barn to the right of the house.

There was no sound except the rustling of some tree leaves. A black and white cat appeared, but kept its distance. The screen door swung open and a woman came down the steps.

As the wagon neared, Lenora recognized Paul Blanton and guessed the other fellow must be Mr. Tetherton. *Well here he comes, finally*, she thought. *Now we'll see what the truth of this is.*

The cat, sitting at her feet, stretched and walked toward the screen door, which opened easily. She headed to the nearest window-well where her new kittens were sleeping. Lenora rose and opened the door.

"Finally made it, huh?" She walked toward the buckboard.

"Yes, sorry I couldn't get here any earlier. I was lucky to get a ride from Pastor Blanton." *She's younger looking than I imagined,* Angus thought.

Lenora nodded. "Hello, Pastor. Well, come on in."

The inside of the house was in stark contrast to the outside façade of painted stucco. The living room décor obviously had a woman's touch.

A wooden sofa and two chairs by the fireplace were covered with brightly-colored quilts. Off the living room was a long wooden dining table with cushion covered benches.

"Want some coffee?"

"Yes, please." Angus started to ask where the bathroom was, but Lenora disappeared into the kitchen.

Paul Blanton seemed to read Angus' mind.

"If you're wondering where the bathroom is, the outhouse is out back." He added with a snicker, "A two-holer, too."

"Thanks," Angus said. "Anything's welcome right now."

"I'll be right behind you, it's been a long ride."

Lenora was pouring out three cups of coffee when they returned.

"Sit down." She motioned toward the two chairs by the fireplace. "You'll stay for supper, Pastor?"

"No, Lenora, thanks. I have to work on my sermon tonight and the Posts have kindly invited me to stay with them. In fact, as soon as I finish this good coffee I should head back. Hate to miss one of your great meals, though."

Angus was glad that Blanton wouldn't be staying, as he wanted to talk to Lenora about the letter as soon as he could and didn't really want someone else listening in. He assumed he was staying overnight, but nothing had been said as yet.

"Sorry to hear that, Pastor, but I'll see you at church tomorrow. Mr. Tetherton, you'll stay of course."

Angus nodded.

"Well then, I'd better be off," Blanton said. Then, addressing Angus, "I'll be staying over Sunday night and going back Monday early, so I assume you'll be coming with me."

"Yes, I think so, but we can talk tomorrow at church."

Lenora's supper was as good as anticipated and Angus was wishing he'd not had the second helping of soup and biscuits. They made small talk during the meal which was mostly Angus answering questions about his trip. Finally, he couldn't put off what had been on his mind all day.

"Can I see the letter now?"

"Yes. Let me clear the table and I'll get everything we found in the steamer trunk."

"Thanks. Here let me help," he said.

Angus had never seen any of the Duncombe letters or envelopes, but Wendell and Oren sent him the complete file, including a transcribed copy of the letter and the Duncombe heir's solution to solving the riddle. He read all the information over several times on the train trip from New York. He learned that the Duncombes were convinced that the treasure left by their father Giles lay somewhere on the property in York. The words on the back of each of the six stamps on William's envelope provided the missing clues to the actual location. At this moment he held that envelope in his hand, and smiled at Lenora.

"Here's what I suggest. I'll tell you all I know and you do the same. Why don't you start," he said.

Lenora told Angus how Lila found the letter and the telegram in the steamer trunk and how her initial reaction was to forget the whole thing. She also told about her and William's reason for leaving England, their family and life in South Dakota.

Angus told her all he knew about the legacy of Giles Duncombe, the riddle and the family's frustration for almost thirty-seven years. He also told her of his father-in-law's long time association with the Duncombe family.

"So this letter has been in the trunk all these years. It's hard to believe," he said. Lenora nodded.

"It's even harder to believe that the treasure may still be hidden away," she said.

"If it is, and this envelope's secret reveals the location, you'll be a rich woman Mrs. Duncan."

"So, what do we do next?"

"We remove the stamps from this envelope and see what's on the other side."

"Simple as that, huh," she said.

"Well, not quite that simple. We have to be very careful."

Lenora put the kettle on at Angus's suggestion and when the water started boiling, he held the envelope over the spout, directing the escaping steam at the six stamps. Slowly, the stamps began to loosen and, being careful not to work too fast, Angus pulled the stamps away from the envelope. When they were off, he laid them face down on a towel.

"Just think, these stamps were put here in 1871," he said. "Let's see if we can read what's on the back."

The words were still legible: *After, This, Hint, To, Help, Remember.*

"So, there you are," Angus said.

"What do they mean?"

"I'm not completely sure, but from what I know, this is the third line of the five line riddle. The Duncombes, especially Giles Jr., and James believe that the first letter of each word form the words that reveal the location."

"Have you seen the rest of the riddle?"

"No. My father-in-law has and perhaps his son Wendell, but I gather the Duncombes have kept that mostly to themselves."

"They've all got to be in their seventies now, don't they? Ben, I mean William, would be sixty-three this year."

"I believe so. And, of course, with the exception of James, they all have grown children and I imagine, grandchildren."

"So, what now, Mr. Tetherton?"

"Angus, please. For now, I'd like to copy down these words, if you've got pen and ink. Then if you don't mind, it's been a long day and I need some time to think about it."

"I understand. I'm a bit tired myself," she said.

Lenora got a piece of paper and the ink pen and then excused herself. When she returned she was carrying some blankets. She picked up a lantern and reached for his hand.

"Come on, I'll show you where you're sleeping."

Angus followed as she went out the back door.

Lenora led him to the barn and over to the hayloft. She stopped by the ladder.

"You'll be very comfortable up there," she said, handing him the blankets. "The well is out in back if you want to wash up or get a drink. Here's a towel for the morning and you know where the outhouse is. I'll leave the lantern with you."

"Thank you. I'm sure I'll be fine."

"Sorry you have to be out here, but country people do talk."

"I quite understand, Lenora. Thank you and I'll see you in the morning."

"Breakfast at seven, church starts at nine and it will take us a while to get there. Goodnight."

Quite a woman, he thought, as she left him and returned to the house.

It was the best sleep he'd had in a long time.

He was shocked when he looked at his pocket watch and saw it was almost six-thirty. *He must look like hell*, he thought. He hadn't shaved in two days and he doubted he would this morning. Shaving in cold water was not something he was looking forward to.

As he neared the back of the house he smelled bacon cooking. He was very hungry. *Must be the country air.*

Lenora was at the stove. "Breakfast will be ready in a few minutes. There's hot water and soap in that pot and a mirror in the hall, in case you want to shave."

"Yes, I think I need to," rubbing the stubble on his face.

She smiled. "Hope you had a good rest."

"I did. The best in many days, thank you."

During breakfast, Angus told Lenora what he thought they should do now. First, he told her to secrete away the paper with the words he had copied from the back of the stamps. He would put the six stamps in the original envelope and take them with him back to New York and then telegraph the words to his father-in-law in England. The next part of his plan caught Lenora off guard.

"I'm going to suggest that you travel to London and be a participant in the discovery."

"What? Even if that would be possible, I can't afford the trip and -----."

Angus anticipated her response. "I'm sure the Duncombes would pay for the trip, and after all, you stand to inherit thousands of dollars. If they agree, we'll wire you the money."

"I couldn't leave the farm and wouldn't want to go by myself."

"I understand that, too. Here's what I think. You pick a traveling companion and then arrange for someone to manage your farm. Don't you have a daughter and son-in-law close?"

At church, Angus met Lila, her husband Jesse Mason and Martha O'Toole. He suggested ahead of time that Lenora invite everyone in the family who was close enough, to dinner. His plan was to tell the family what he and Lenora had discussed. Then, before they left the church, he confirmed to Pastor Blanton that he would travel back to Philip with him on Monday.

"I'll be by to get you at seven and we'll try and get back in one day," Blanton had told him.

They reached Philip just before dark and Angus checked into the Seneschal. The train for Pierre left at 9:14 in the morning, so after having supper with Pastor Blanton, he thanked him for all he had done and retired for the night.

There were only three men having breakfast in the dining room when Angus entered and he thought he recognized the older one from his previous stay. The man looked up when Angus sat at a nearby table.

"Good morning," the man said.

"Good morning. You were here last Friday." Angus said, rhetorically.

"Yes I was. You're very observant," he said. "Care to join me?"

"Why, yes, but you've almost finished."

"That's all right, I've plenty of time before my train leaves and I'd enjoy the company," he said.

"You must be taking the 9:14 to Pierre too," said Angus.

"Yes, I am. Caine's the name, Allan Caine."

"Nice to meet you," said Angus as he sat down. "Angus Tetherton."

"So what brings you to Philip, Angus?" he asked.

"Just helping some people in the country with some financial matters," Angus said. "How about you?"

"Oh, just visiting a relative."

They engaged in small talk, mostly about the weather, while Caine finished his coffee and Angus ate his ham and eggs. *He's got a definite English accent*, thought Angus. *Funny he's not said anything about mine.*

"Well, I'd best check out myself. Nice talking to you and maybe we'll see each other on the train. Do you have a compartment?"

"Yes, compartment 5A," Angus said. "Come join me when you get a chance, I'd enjoy the company."

"Thanks, I will." Caine rose and they shook hands.

This is going to be easier than I imagined, he thought to himself. *He doesn't suspect a thing. As his friend Jacques in Toronto would say, 'Just like shooting fish in a barrel.'* He quickly packed and returned to the lobby. The clerk looked up as he approached.

"Here's my key and I'll settle my bill now."

"Yes, Mr. Caine. Hope you have a pleasant trip to Pierre."

"Oh, I'm sure I will," he said.

It was shortly after ten in the morning when there was a knock on the door of compartment 5A. "Yes," Angus said.

"It's Allan Caine."

"Come in, please," said Angus. "Have a seat."

"Thanks," Caine said and sat down opposite Angus. "So, are you going on to Sioux Falls?"

"Yes, and then on to Minneapolis where I get the train for Chicago and New York. How about you?"

"I'm going as far as Chicago," Caine said.

"Then we'll be seeing each other often, I suspect," said Angus.

"Yes, I imagine. Listen, I've got some work to do, but why don't we have dinner together. We should be arriving in Pierre about that time," Caine said. He rose to shake Angus's hand. As Caine reached out with his right hand, his left hand rose in a sweeping arc above Angus's head.

"Mr. Tetherton! Mr. Tetherton!"

Angus heard someone calling his name, but didn't seem to have the strength to rise. *Where was he?* His head hurt and he sensed he was lying down. The voice came again.

"Mr. Tetherton. We're in Pierre."

Angus got to his knees and pulled himself onto the compartment seat. He saw the blood on his hand and on the seat. His valise was on the floor by the window.

"Yes, come in. I've been hurt."

One look at Angus and the porter departed to get some help. Angus tried to reconstruct what had happened, but he was still very dizzy. He did recall Caine's arm swinging down on him and then nothing. *My god, he hit me!*

The porter returned with the conductor and some first aid supplies. "Sir, you've fallen and have a nasty gash on your head. We should take you off the train and have you checked at the nearest hospital," the conductor said.

Angus remembered that they were in Pierre. *I've been out for at least an hour*, he thought.

"No, no, I'll be all right. Just help me clean-up and if you've got some gauze and a bandage, I need that."

"Are you sure, sir?" the porter said.

He decided that, for now, he'd let them continue to believe he had fallen. "By the way, a Mr. Allan Caine and I were going to have dinner together. Have you seen him?"

"Why yes, he got off the train shortly after we got here."

"How long ago was that?" Angus asked.

"About ten minutes ago," said the conductor.

"Thanks, I'll be fine now, How long before we depart?"

"In fifteen minutes." After they left his compartment, Angus checked through the valise and his coat pockets. Everything was there in the valise, but after rechecking all his pockets he knew what was missing. *The letter. Damn. He took the letter! But Why? How did he even know?*

Chapter Thirteen

Birmingham, England – April 1908

They read the telegram again, almost in disbelief. It was short, but left little doubt in the sender's meaning.

Have information we sought. ATHTHR. Will arrive, S S Liverpool, South Hampton, April 16.

It was signed by the name he now used.

"So, what do you think?"

"I think with your mother's help we can now solve the puzzle."

"He's mighty trusting. We could just go ahead without him, you know," he said.

"No. It's only because of him that we have what we need. We owe him that," she said. "Besides, your mother has the rest of the riddle."

"She's also the one who learned about the letter being found," he said.

"Yes. So, I suggest we go to her right away and see if together we can solve the riddle, and then we'll be ready when he gets here."

London, England - April 1908

Wendell read the telegram from Angus and the one from the New York office and went to see his father. Oren finished the first one quickly.

"And he has no idea who Caine is?" Oren said, in disbelief.

"No, he'd just met him at the hotel and then on the train. Angus is lucky he wasn't hurt more than a good lump on the head," said Wendell.

"What about the puzzle words?"

"Here's the second telegram," said Wendell.

The telegram from New York advised that they heard from Angus, he was all right and that he was scheduled to arrive back in New York in three days. Further, that he remembered the puzzle words and would send them directly by telegram to Wendell during his layover in Chicago. Wendell and Oren would have to decide how and when to give the information to the Duncombes. Finally, he recommended that the Duncombes be apprised of the theft and warned of the probability that someone likely has enough information now to find the treasure before the family does.

"So, we should be getting the telegram with the words soon," Oren said.

"Yes. Likely sometime tomorrow," Wendell answered. "What do you suggest we do as far as the Duncombes are concerned?"

Oren did not hesitate. "The sooner we contact them the better. I'd set up a meeting with James as soon as you get the telegram from Chicago. Also, have him wire the rest of the family and set up a meeting at your office. I'll attend, too. I'd guess that the earliest the family meeting would take place would be in two days."

South Hampton, England – April 16, 1908

It had been years since he'd seen him. *How old was he now?* He thought back to those years in London. *Probably in his early sixties.* He continued to scan the passengers leaving customs. Then there he was. His hair was almost completely gray and he walked somewhat stooped over, but there was no doubt it was Edward Keith. Then it occurred to him, that he might not be recognizable either. He hurried over to meet him.

"Edward," he said extending his hand.

"It's Allan Caine now, remember." He ignored Henry's offered handshake.

"Yes, sorry. Can I help you with your bags?"

"Fine," Caine said. "You're by yourself?"

"Yes, we'll meet her at the hotel. I got us rooms for tonight."

During dinner they brought Caine up to date on what they had done since receiving his telegram. Caine didn't add much to the conversation and seemed reluctant to offer any details about his trip to South Dakota and his encounter with Angus Tetherton. When asked a second time about how he got the letter, he glared at them and rose.

"These things are best discussed in private, so I suggest you finish up," Cain said. "I'm going to my room and you can meet me there in ten minutes. It's room 301."

"Charming fellow," she said after he left.

In the privacy of his room, Caine seemed more relaxed, but left no time zeroing in on the purpose of their meeting.

"So, have you tried to solve the puzzle?"

"Yes, and I think we have the answer," he said. "If we go on the premise that the first letter of each word forms other words, then the six letters you got from Tetherton fill in the third group. Everyone's probably figured that the first word is York, the second Home, the third is Of, the sixth Up, the seventh is Four and the eighth is Left. Now we have the fourth and fifth."

"Which are?" said Caine.

"Death and Three. Here, I've written out what I think is the whole riddle." He handed Caine the paper while Olivia looked on.

Allan Caine stared at it for a long time. "What do you suppose is the meaning of 'Home Of Death?'"

For the first time in a while, she spoke up.

"At first that stumped me, but then I remembered mother talking about their trips to York. It's what they called the family mausoleum when they were children."

"At the farm in York?" he said. She nodded.

"But hasn't the York farm been assumed to be the primary location for years?" He didn't wait for an answer. "That was guessed back in 1871 and I'm sure the family has searched everything that even remotely could be a hiding place."

Olivia answered. "Yes, they have, but quite obviously, if the treasure is in the mausoleum, they didn't fine it."

Caine bowed slightly. "You are correct, of course. Then I suggest we get to London, pick up your mother and head to York before the rest of the Duncombes figure this out. Is your mother expecting us?"

"Yes she is," Henry said.

As soon as they got back to their room, Henry took Olivia in his arms and neither said anything for several minutes. Finally Olivia pulled back.

"I hope we're doing the right thing," she said.

"You still have doubts, then?"

"I do. I know that you and your mother have strong feelings about being cheated out of any inheritance, and I know we'll need the money when we marry and go to Canada. However, I just don't trust Keith, or I mean, Caine."

"So, what should we do, wait until you inherit from your parents?" he said. "They'll cut you off when they learn about me."

It was an argument they'd had before. Henry pulled her close again and gently stroked her hair. Olivia relaxed and turned her face upward to meet his eyes.

"I know, but I still feel guilty," she said.

Henry released one arm and cupped her face in his hand, then bent slightly to kiss her. Olivia eagerly returned his kiss.

"It's late, I know," he said.

"It's never too late," she said, and followed him to their bed.

In his room, the conspiring Allan Caine poured himself a whiskey from his pocket flask and contemplated tomorrow's trip. *It will be interesting to see Anne again after all these years. Maybe he'd let her live, but Henry and that little snip, Olivia, that was something else.*

Oren was in the London office when Wendell arrived just after eight.

"Had your morning coffee?"

"Yes," Oren answered.

"They should be here by nine o'clock," Wendell said. "Let's go into the conference room. I've told Marion to show them in as they arrive."

First to get there were James and Madeline, then Giles and Ruth with their son Michael, then Terrance and Evelyn with Stephen and just after nine, Mary and Tyler.

"It looks like we're missing Sarah and Olivia, as far as the immediate family goes," Oren said.

"Sarah choose to stay home in York," Giles said.

"We haven't been able to contact Olivia," Mary said.

"All right then, let's get started," said Wendell. "Father and I know that you've all tried, over the years, to solve at least some of the puzzle and that the farm in York is the likely location. What you haven't been able to discern is the exact location. The information from my brother-in-law Angus should provide the missing links. Giles, as the eldest, I suggest you take over from here. Oh, and one more thing, as we advised earlier, there's a good chance that someone else has the solution by now, so time is of the essence."

Wendell rose to leave and motioned for his father to follow.

"Wait," said Giles, "you've been so involved in all this, especially you Oren, that I think the family will agree with me, that we want you to stay and be a part of this."

"Yes," said James. Terrance and Mary also voiced their consent.

"Very well. Let's get this thing solved," said Oren.

"So that's it. After all these years," said Terrance. "Here, I'll write the whole thing down." When he finished he handed the paper to Giles.

You'll Only Reap Kindled Haste. Or
Make Each One's First Delight. Even
After This Hint To Help. Remember
Eden's Eve Used Place First. One
Urges Regarding Letter Each Found There.

"Taking the first letters of each word, you have this," said Terrance, handing Giles a second piece of paper.

York Home Of Death Three Up Four Left

"Does that mean anything to any of you?" asked Wendell.

"It sure does," said Terrance. "Home of Death is what we called the family mausoleum. I'd also guess that *three up four left,* is the specific location."

"But from where?" said James.

"Giles, you live there now. What do you think, you always were the one to solve father's riddles?"

"It must be one of the niches or wall crypts. We'll just have to go there and see," Giles said.

"When do Lenora and her sister get here?" said Ruth.

"Their ship docks in two days, but we can't wait that long," said James.

"No, you can't," said Oren. "My suggestion is that you all go ahead and make arrangements to go to York. Wendell will go with you. I will meet Lenora and arrange for her and her sister to get there as soon as possible."

"That sounds reasonable," Mary said.

It had been many years, but Oren recognized Clarence Franklin right away.

"Mr. Franklin. How are you?"

At first Clarence hesitated, then recognition took over and he rose with his hand extended. "Mr. Eflow. It's been a long time."

"Yes, it has. Mrs. Franklin not with you?"

"No, Bertha isn't that well and just couldn't make the trip from Winsford."

"Sorry to hear that. Any sign of your daughters yet?"

"No, but the ship's been in for some time, so they should be clearing customs any time now," he said.

"You must be very excited. How long has it been?" said Wendell.

"Almost thirty-six years. A lifetime," said Clarence.

While they waited, Oren explained about the trip to York that he and Wendell arranged for Lenora and Martha.

"Sorry you're visit will be so brief, but after this is all over, I'm sure your daughters will spend some time with you in Winsford."

"Yes, Martha said in her wire that they would be with us for a week before going back. At least I have tonight with them," he said.

"You should get into London early enough today to have a nice dinner and visit," Oren said. We have rooms for you and your daughters at the Charlton and we'll pick them up at seven thirty tomorrow morning."

Just then a group of passengers came through the doors.

Though father and daughters hadn't been together in thirty-six years, the regular exchange of photographs made it easy for Lenora and Martha to spot their father. Clarence also recognized his daughters and rushed to meet them. Oren watched as the three held each other. Clarence, now well into his eighties, looked small and frail surrounded by the two robust, countrywomen, but Oren noticed that he seemed to be squeezing them as hard as they were him.

He walked over to join the threesome.

"Lenora, Martha, I'm Oren Eflow. Welcome back to England."

"Thank you, and thanks for all your help in getting us here," said Lenora, releasing her hold and extending her hand.

"That goes for me too," said Martha. "How much time do we have before we leave for York?"

"Actually, we're going to London first, where you'll spend the night with your father and then the two of you will catch the 8:30 to York from Charing Cross station," said Oren.

"You're not going?" said Martha.

"No. Wendell will be in York and help as much as he can, and I'll stay home in London." He looked at Clarence. "You know, some of us are getting up in years." Clarence nodded, and smiled.

"So, I suggest we gather up your luggage and head for the station. The next train to London is in twenty minutes," Oren said.

On the ride to London, Oren brought the sisters up to date by telling them about the Duncombe family meeting. The suppositions were about the mausoleum and about the very real danger being that a person or persons likely unknown to them may have already solved the puzzle.

"Ben fondly recalled the family excursions to York," Lenora said, and then continued. "Do you think the man who attacked Mr. Tetherton is over here?"

"He very well may be, but my guess is that he is working with someone in England," said Oren.

"But who would have known about the letters and the riddle left by Ben's father except someone in the family?" said Lenora.

"That's true," said Oren.

"But, any family member would share in the hidden treasure, wouldn't they," offered Martha.

"Yes they would, and that's a puzzle in itself," Oren said.

Chapter Fourteen

Giles and Ruth Duncombe moved to the York farm after he retired from the College in 1899. During the years since he inherited the farm, Giles had either been on sabbaticals or lived in college housing. Though his father's will stipulated the Fitzworths be retained for only five years, the Duncombe family had now employed three generations of Fitzworths. Jasper's grandson, Oliver, currently managed the farm and lived in a nearby cottage provided by the Duncombes. Oliver's father John managed the farm after his father Jasper died in 1875.

Oliver's sister Dorothy came twice a week on Mondays and Fridays to clean the Duncombe house and her brother's cottage. Oliver, now fifty-seven, had never married. He hadn't fully recovered from a childhood riding accident and walked bent over, and lacked strength in his left arm, but otherwise was as strong as an ox. His only weakness was his fondness for a few pints at the local pubs, and it showed in his waistline.

When there was a Duncombe family gathering or when the Duncombes had overnight guests, Dorothy helped Ruth with the food and room preparations.

The first day in York, Allan Caine and Henry learned what they needed to know about the Duncombe farm without raising suspicions. Giles and his wife were in London and the manager, Mr. Fitzworth, spent his evenings in local pubs.

That evening, Allan, Anne Spencer, Henry Spencer and Olivia Franklin cautiously walked up the road from the gate and made their way to the mausoleum.

"Anne, you and Olivia keep watch while Henry and I go into the mausoleum," Caine said.

The family mausoleum was constructed with an Egyptian motif. The structure was square, with a flat roof and four ornate column capitals on each side. Above the doorway was a winged scarab. The door itself was massive and just to the right of the door was etched a verse from the William Henley poem, *The Invictus.*

> *Beyond this place of wrath and tears*
> *Looms but the horror of the shade,*
> *And yet the menace of the years*
> *Finds, and shall find me, unafraid.*

Inside, the left wall was blank, except for a few family pictures. To the right were the wall niches for urn placement and twenty wall crypts.

In the center was a long, narrow marble table and this is where Allan told Henry to place their lantern.

"All right. So, the verse says, *three up, four left,*" Caine said.

"There's only two columns of urn niches," said Henry.

"Then the location directions must have to do with the crypts," Caine said. "Now the question is which column to start at."

"The crypts are four high and five wide, so counting from the bottom right hand corner----." Henry counted three up and then four left and arrived at a crypt that, according to the inscription on the plaque, contained the remains of Milton Duncombe, who died in 1831.

"That must be Giles senior's father," Henry said. "You wouldn't think he'd hide something in there."

"The only other possibility is if you start at the second column, rather that the first," said Caine. "Try that."

"This door plaque has the inscription for Melville Fuller, 1834-1835," Henry said, after again counting three up and four left. "Must have been the infant son of one of Milton's married daughters."

"Let's try that one first," Cain said.

The thick door of the crypt opened with some effort to reveal a small casket. Caine removed the casket and shined his lantern inside the crypt. Nothing else was inside.

"Open this up," Caine said, motioning to the small casket.

"I don't like this," said Henry. He was remembering images, long forgotten, of burial details in the Boer War.

"We have no choice."

The lid to the casket came loose with little labor and Caine swung it back on its hinges. Inside were the skeletal remains of a small child. It appeared to have been wrapped in a blanket, now mostly rotted away. Caine reached in and felt around the remains. Finding nothing of interest, he examined the inside of the casket for any places of concealment. He tapped on the bottom, the sides and the top, but the sounds only confirmed that there were no obvious hollow spots.

While this was going on, Henry stood to one side, and then unable to hold back anymore, turned around and vomited.

"Why don't you go outside and get some air and check on the women," Caine said. "And get something to clean up your mess, while you're at it."

This is all I need, he thought, *someone with a weak stomach.*

While Henry was gone, Allan checked around inside the casket again. Finding nothing, he closed the top and placed it back in the crypt.

I'll need some help for the next one, he thought.

The door of the crypt came open easily and revealed the end of a casket. In the dim light, Allan could see the handle. He tugged and confirmed his earlier thought.

At first, when Henry went outside, he didn't see the women standing in the shadows between the columns and the outside wall of the mausoleum. They watched Henry walk back up the road toward their carriage. There had been no signs of anyone on the main road and to fill the time, Olivia was telling Anne more about their plans for Canada and her increasing concern about what they were doing that evening.

"Wonder where Henry's going?" said Anne.

"Should we call to him?" Olivia said.

"No, he'll be back, I suspect."

"Here he comes now." Olivia stepped out of the shadows. "Please don't tell him about my doubts, I know he feels strongly about this," she said.

"As do I," Anne said.

As Anne stepped out to join Olivia, they heard Allan call from inside that he needed some help. She called to her son.

"Henry, come on, Allan needs our help."

"Quiet, mother, you don't know who could be around. I thought I saw a light over at the caretaker's cottage."

"What were you doing?"

"Getting some air and something to clean up a mess," he said. "It's not a pleasant task in there, as you're about to discover."

As he got closer, they could smell the vomit on him, but before they said anything, they heard Allan calling again.

"Sorry, Henry," said Olivia.

Allan called a third time, much louder.

"Let's go," said Henry, " before he wakes the dead."

They found Allan leaning against the table.

"It's about time. Come on, it will take all of us to pull this casket out and lower it onto the table."

Allan was correct, but after several tugs and one final pull, the casket came out and they were able to set it on the table.

Anne shut the heavy crypt door and noticed for the first time the brass nameplate.

"Milton Duncombe. Who was that?" Anne said.

"Henry thinks it's Giles's grandfather," said Allan.

"That's right. Milton was my great grandfather," Olivia said. She walked a few steps away and beckoned to Henry. "Henry, I'm still not feeling right about this," she said quietly. " Maybe we should forget this and leave now."

Allan Caine couldn't help but notice. "Is there a problem?"

Henry turned back. "No!"

"All right, then, help me loosen this lid and maybe you'll feel better Olivia when you see the treasure that must be inside."

The lid came free with minimal prying and revealed the remains of whom they assumed was Milton Duncombe.

"Seventy seven years and he doesn't look a day over thirty," said Henry.

"Henry, that's not funny," said Anne. "After all, he's your great grandfather too."

"Yes, but I'll never get the right to claim him, will I."

"Come on, stop the bickering and lend a hand," said Allan.

But, they found nothing unusual. No hidden treasure, only decaying clothes and what was left of Milton Duncombe.

Allan went through the same regimen of searching and tapping he had done on the small casket even after the others had given up any hope. Twenty minutes later, he too stepped back in disgust.

"Now what?" said Anne.

"It's got to be here," said Allan.

"Unless we were wrong about the mausoleum," Henry said.

"What if the old goat played a final trick on everyone and reversed the order?" said Allan.

"What do you mean?" Henry said.

Allan explained that perhaps Giles's directions were reversed on purpose and they should try four up and three left.

Anne looked at the wall crypts. "But Allan, there are no plates on any of the crypts in the top row. They're probably all empty."

"That's the point, my dear, he probably hid the treasure in an empty one. Come on, let's open up that one," he said, indicating the door three over in the top row.

The door opened easily to reveal an empty crypt. Henry directed the light about and Allan once again checked the walls, but there were no signs of any opening for concealing something and the walls appeared solid, as before.

Allan went over to the casket of Milton Duncombe and taking hold of the handle, slammed the lid closed.

"Damn!"

Olivia tugged at Henry's sleeve and pulled him aside. "Henry, it's time to go," she whispered.

Allan overheard. "Nobody's going anywhere."

Henry, though, was ready to heed Olivia's request. "Allan, it's over. We're going before it gets light and we're caught here. Mother, are you coming with us?"

Anne went to Allan. "He's right, Edward," using his real name. "I believe that either we guessed wrong or somebody found the treasure before. I have a gut feeling, though, that it was never here."

Henry stepped forward. "Come on, Allan, it's time to go." He walked over to the casket. Let's at least put this back in the crypt."

But Allan Caine made no move to help. Instead he looked menacingly at his three cohorts.

"I'm not leaving yet, and neither are any of you."

"Yes we are, Allan," said Anne, with conviction.

As she turned to leave, Allan reached out to pull her back, but Henry grabbed his arm and shoved him back.

"That's it, Allan. You lay another hand on my mother and - --."

"And what. You fool. Don't you want a share of what's rightfully yours. You're just a dolt like your uncle William was."

Allan rushed at Henry, but Henry, despite his bad leg, was much quicker.

"I told you to back off," Henry said, and hit Allan squarely on the jaw.

Allan at first didn't seem to feel the effect of the blow, but then his eyes rolled back and he fell to the floor, just missing the edge of the table.

"Let's go," Henry said to Anne and Olivia.

"What about the casket and Allan?" Olivia said.

Anne bent over Allan. "He's out cold, but otherwise all right, I think."

"When he wakes up, the casket will be his problem. Come on, it's starting to get light and I, for one, don't want to be here any longer," he said. Henry took Olivia's hand and walked out the door. He hesitated and turned back. His mother was still kneeling by Allan. "Mother, are you coming?"

"We just can't leave him here."

"Mother, he'd leave you in the same circumstances."

Anne Spencer rose, hesitated briefly, and then followed her son. "Henry, I'm sorry. I should never have gotten you involved."

"It was as much my idea as yours. Olivia was right. I should have listened to her a long time ago."

Oliver Fitzworth got back from the King William pub at half past midnight and after a night of downing many pints, he fell into bed and was soon fast asleep. About six he was awakened by what he thought was the sound of horses. He got to his bedroom window just in time to see a carriage going through the gate and turning north toward the city. *Now who was that?* he thought. *The Duncombes weren't due until this afternoon, and besides, the carriage was leaving, not coming. What's going on?*

Oliver splashed some water on his face, pulled his boots on over his long-johns, and went out onto his small porch. By now the carriage was out of sight. *Better check the house.*

As he approached the house he noticed light coming from the open door of the mausoleum. *Now that's odd*, he thought. Then, when he was just a few paces from the door, a man appeared, and seeing Oliver, ran toward the road.

"Stop!" Oliver called, but the man ignored him and picked up his pace.

Oliver also increased his pace, and though still feeling the effects of a night of revelry, caught up in short order.

Then with a lunge he caught the man by the back of his jacket and pulled him down. As the man fell, however, he rolled into a sitting position and just as fast, a knife appeared in his hand.

"Back off you lummox, or you'll wish you hadn't," he said.

Oliver had been in many a brawl in his lifetime and the little man with the knife seemingly held no fear for him. He picked up a nearby tree branch with his right hand. "Oh, a knife. Let's just see what you've got, you little pipsqueak. Call me a lummox, will you."

The York railway station was moved from Toft Green to its present location near Micklegate Bar in 1899. To reach the Duncombe farm, they would cross the Ouse River, using the Lendal Bridge. Giles remembered crossing the river by ferry as a boy, before the bridge was built.

Michael had driven their carriage in and left it at Bonham's Livery on Blake Street. There would be room for his father and mother, the Franklins and Wendell. James, Madeline, Terrance, Evelyn and Stephen would follow in a rented carriage.

While looking out the passenger window, Mary said, "York hasn't changed that much since I was last here."

"Oh, but it has, you just don't see it yet. Wait till we get closer into the city," said Ruth, joining her. "You remember that Sweet Shop on Coney Street?"

"Yes," said Mary. "Joseph's or something like that."

"It was Joseph Terry's. Well, now it's a bookstore. And, the old fire station on Shamblee is a furniture warehouse."

"Things do change," Mary said.

The train slowed and the platform came into view.

"Isn't that Oliver, Giles?" Ruth said. "I thought he was going to stay out at the farm."

Giles joined his wife and Mary at the window.

"Why, it is, and that's Constable Davis with him. I hope everything's all right," Giles said.

Giles disembarked first and waved at Oliver, who had seen him and was already walking his way.

"Oliver, has something happened?"

"Yes sir, we've got a bit of a problem at the farm. I'll help Michael with your things while the Constable explains."

"What's so serious you two had to meet us here?" said Giles to the Constable.

Miles Davis had always been somewhat intimidated by Giles Duncombe, so he phrased his response carefully and came right to the point.

"There's been a death and a break-in at your farm."

"My God."

Ruth, Terrance, James and Wendell Eflow joined Giles.

"What is it, Giles?" Ruth said.

"It seems there's been some kind of accident and a break-in at the farm," he said.

"It was no accident, Mr. Duncombe," said Constable Davis.

"Not an accident! Well, let's hear the details, and before you start, you should meet our investigator, Mr. Eflow, from London. Perhaps he can assist you."

Wendell extended his hand to Davis. "Glad to help any way I can."

"From London, my my, but I think we have everything under control," Davis said. "Mr. Duncombe can ride with Oliver and me, and we'll explain on the way to the farm. Mr. Eflow, you can join us. My man Jensen will drive."

180

"I had no choice, sir, it was either him or me."

Oliver had just finished his accounting of the incident and the ensuing fight with the man caught leaving the mausoleum.

"I quite understand, Oliver," said Giles. "Any idea who he is, or was, I suppose?"

"Name's Allan Caine, according to the Canadian passport he had on him," said Davis.

"Isn't that the name of the person who attacked your brother-in-law Angus, Wendell? Giles said.

"Yes, it is. A Canadian passport. That's interesting," said Wendell. "Any other identification?"

"No, but I did find something odd stuffed in his jacket pocket."

"What's that?" said Giles.

"He had an old envelope addressed to a W. Duncombe."

"Do you have it with you?" Wendell asked.

"As a matter of fact, I do."

He removed an envelope from his coat. "Be careful, there's some loose stamps inside. Old ones, too, by the looks of them."

"This has got to be the letter that he took from Angus," said Wendell removing the stamps. "Look, these have words on the back, just like all the others."

Wendell could tell that Davis was about to ask a question, but Giles interrupted.

"What more can you tell us about the damage in the mausoleum?" asked Giles.

"Not much that I haven't said. It looked like he broke into at least two of the crypts, and how he got the one casket out by himself, I don't know."

"Maybe he wasn't alone," said Wendell.

James was handling the reins in one of the following carriages. Stephen was sitting beside him.

"How long has it been since you've been here Uncle James?"

"Oh, at least a year. Madeline and I visited Giles and Ruth over the holidays. Let's see, that would be about sixteen months ago."

They continued to make idle conversation as the carriage continued up Low Petergate and made the turn to access Lendal Bridge.

"How long before we're there?" said Madeline, calling up.

"Another fifteen to twenty minutes should do it," James said.

"I wonder who the dead fellow is?" said Stephen.

"I'm sure the Constable will figure that out," James said. "I'm more worried about the condition of the mausoleum."

"Oliver must have really walloped the fellow hard," Stephen said.

"Well, I suspect you would have too if someone came at you with a knife," said James.

"Here's the turn to the road, Uncle James, we're almost there," said Stephen.

Handling the reins in the last carriage, Tyler Franklin also saw the approaching turn and yelled down to Mary. "We're getting close."

"Well, maybe we'll find out what's going on now," Mary said to Evelyn.

"I sincerely hope so."

The lead carriage with Giles, Oliver Fitzworth, Constable Davis and Wendell Eflow was driven by one of the Constable's men, Thomas Jensen, and he stopped the carriage at the main entrance to the house. Dorothy Brunswick, Oliver's sister, came out the door to greet them.

"Come in and clean up and have some tea, you'll need it for what's ahead," Dorothy said.

"You can offer the tea to the ladies, Mrs. Brunswick, but we'll be going out to the mausoleum," said Constable Davis.

"Is that where this Allan Caine is?" said Giles.

"No, we've moved his body into the barn, but I thought you'd better take a look at the damage first. He'll keep for a while," said Davis.

Soon they were joined by Terrance, James, Tyler, Mary and Stephen.

"Stephen, I know you'd like to come along, but right now, I'd appreciate if you'd help Michael with the luggage and get everyone settled," said Terrance.

"Very well, Constable, you lead the way," said Giles.

All matter of things, including pieces of material, some bones, a lantern and several tools, including a pry bar surrounded the casket of Milton Duncombe. The crypt door stood open, but the casket was closed.

"Besides this one, it looks like he opened one of the other crypts. See here," Davis said, pointing to the crypt of Melville Fuller. "The rest appear undisturbed. The question is, what was he after?"

"We can answer that question, I believe," said Giles.

During the carriage ride, Wendell had correctly sensed the Duncombes' reluctance to discuss the legacy of their father with Davis and the fact that the mausoleum may hold the treasure, so he had said nothing. Now, he listened to Giles and the others explain to Constable Davis about the hidden treasure and the puzzle clues to a location in the mausoleum.

"So, you think this Allan Caine was searching for the treasure?" said Davis.

"Yes, and as you found nothing on him other than his papers and the envelope, I'd assume he found nothing."

"How about the grounds around where Oliver and Caine fought?" said Mary.

"That's a good point, Mrs. Franklin, I took a quick look-see, but I'll have Thomas go over that area again to be sure," Davis said. Then hesitating, "What would he be looking for?"

"That, I am afraid to say, we don't know," said James. He walked over to the wall crypts. "But, I do know this, our Mr. Caine seems to have been searching in the two possible locations from our puzzle. Look, if you start in the first column and go three up and four over you arrive at the crypt of Milton Duncombe. His casket now lies on this table."

"Yes, and if you start at the bottom of the second column, you get to Melville Fuller," Terrance said.

"We obviously need to do our own search and check all the possibilities, before we jump to any conclusions," said Giles.

"I quite agree," said Wendell, "but perhaps we'd better take a look at the body, so Constable Davis can get on with his job."

"Good idea," said Davis, "why don't you follow me over to the barn."

"Mrs. Franklin, perhaps you'd like to excuse yourself."

"No, thank you, Constable, I'll be quite all right."

"Wow, you certainly whacked him, Oliver," said James.

"Yes sir, I did, but didn't have much choice in the matter," Oliver said. His blow had put a large dent in the left side of the head, just below the ear, but even with a shattered jaw, the facial features of the dead man were still basically intact.

"Anyone recognize him?" said Davis.

Terrance stared long and hard at the crumpled figure. *I know this fellow from somewhere,* he thought. He searched his memory, but came up blank. Maybe years ago. There was something familiar, but he just couldn't recall what it was.

Everyone answered but Terrance.

"Terrance," said Mary.

"There is something, but I just can't, -----."

"Terrance?"

"My god, I think that's Edward Keith!"

"The man who swindled William?" asked Giles.

"Yes, I'm almost positive now, but Lenora and Martha should be able to recognize him too," said Terrance, "he's their cousin."

"How did you know him, Terrance?" said Giles.

"That's a long story, Giles, and for another time, but needless to say, I had dealings with him years ago. Not good dealings either, I'm sorry to say."

"My father can add to that, I'm sure," said Wendell. "He tried to find Keith for years."

"Yes, I remember the tales of the infamous Mr. Keith, though I never met him," said James.

"When do Lenora and Martha arrive, Wendell?" said James.

"Their ship docked today, so I'd expect them no later than

the noon train tomorrow," said Wendell. "Too bad father's not coming, he'd be surprised about Edward Keith."

"Speaking of Mr. Caine, or Keith, as you suspect, Thomas and I will be taking him into the morgue now. So whoever is meeting the two sisters may want to stop by there before coming out here tomorrow," said Constable Davis. "As for the mausoleum situation, I'll leave that for you to handle."

"I'll be meeting them," said Wendell.

"Very well then, Thomas and I will remove the body and be on our way," said Davis. "I'll expect to see you at station sometime around noon then, Mr. Eflow."

After the Constable and Jensen departed, the men and Mary joined the rest of the family and in short order brought everyone up to date.

"So you don't think this Caine fellow found the hidden treasure?" said Madeline.

"No, we don't, but we're still assuming there was something there to find," said James.

"I don't understand," said Ruth.

Giles turned to his wife. "We don't really know for sure that where Caine looked was even correct. If it was, and he didn't find anything, then if there was something there once, it's gone now." Ruth looked perplexed at his explanation.

"However," added Terrance, "until we look for ourselves, using the puzzle solution, we can't be sure. But from what I saw, Keith, or Caine, as he now calls himself, appears to have looked in the same places we would have."

"We need to go back to the mausoleum and see what we can find," said Madeline.

"Yes, my dear, you observe correctly," said Terrance.

"Let's go then," said Giles, who obviously liked his renewed role as the family leader.

"You all go ahead," said Ruth. "I'll stay here with Dorothy and get things ready for this evening."

"I'd just as soon stay also," said Madeline.

"Me, too. You all go ahead," said Evelyn.

The rest followed Giles back to the mausoleum, except at Giles's suggestion, Oliver stayed to help unload the rest of everyone's luggage.

"We've got several hours of daylight left, so let's put our heads together and see what we can come up with," said Giles.

"What about the casket?" said James, pointing to the table.

"Let's leave it where it is, for now," said Giles. "My suggestion is that we start from scratch, assuming everything is as it was before Mr. Caine arrived."

For the next thirty minutes they tried all the conceivable combinations of directions using the puzzle solution. In the end, however, they ended up exactly as Caine had with two locations; either the crypt of the child, Melville Fuller, or Milton Duncombe.

"Three up and four left from the first column is the crypt for the casket of Milton Duncombe," said Terrance, "which I believe is the most logical location. Stephen, James, give me a hand."

The lid came open quite easily. "Caine must have already had this open," said Stephen.

"Yes, I suspect so," said James. "Come on Michael, give us a hand at searching inside. What a mess!"

Michael reluctantly did so, but even with the four of them feeling and tapping all about, nothing was found.

"Tyler, you, Mary and Giles search inside the crypt," said Terrance. "Check for any possible hiding places."

Nothing was found in the crypt or in the casket. James and Stephen even tried to pry loose the walls of the casket, but they were solid.

"Shall we leave the casket here?" said Michael.

"No, let's put it back in the crypt," Giles said. "Stephen, why don't you and your father open up the child's crypt and see what's to be found while we're putting this away."

The search of the infant's casket and crypt had the same results. Nothing was found that in any way related to a missing treasure.

"Michael, please go get a lantern, it's getting hard to see," said Giles to his son.

"Shouldn't we just wait until tomorrow, Giles?" James asked. "I think we've about exhausted all our ideas for today and I am getting hungry and could use a good drink."

"I agree with James," said Mary. "We need to rethink this whole puzzle in the light of day, and I too am ready for a cold ale and some food."

"I don't want to put a damper on everyone's hopes, but one possibility is that the treasure was here and it's now gone," said Tyler.

"That's entirely possible," said Giles. "All right, I agree, let's call it a day. An ale sounds great. Who knows, maybe Lenora and her sister will have some fresh ideas when they get here."

Chapter Fifteen

Michael Duncombe accompanied Wendell to the station to meet Lenora and Martha's train, which arrived on time. Neither man had met the sisters, and they were relying on some recent pictures provided by Oren. They need not have worried, however, as the sisters' dress and tanned complexions set them apart from the typical English women that departed the train.

"Mrs. Duncan, a pleasure to meet you, I'm Wendell Eflow, and this must be Martha," he said, extending his hand first to Lenora, then Martha.

Michael stood to one side, not at first knowing what to say. Lenora turned to face him.

"I'm guessing you're a Duncombe, probably Michael," she said.

"Yes," he said. "Giles's son. I guess I should call you Aunt Lenora, although you don't seem that much older than I."

"Ah, a flatterer, just like his uncle, huh Lenora," said Martha. "Hello, if you haven't guessed, I'm Martha, Martha O'Toole." She offered her hand to each of the men.

"You may call me aunt or just Lenora. Lenora will be fine, Michael."

"How was your voyage and train trip?" Wendell asked.

"It was quite thrilling, actually, especially getting to see our father yesterday," said Lenora. "However, we're glad to be here."

"I understand," said Wendell. "So, let's get your luggage and on the way to the farm, Michael and I will bring you up to date and you can tell us more about your trip. We do, however, have one stop to make in York first."

Lenora held the envelope and the letter in one hand and the six postage stamps in the other.

"Thank you for these, they mean a lot to me," she said.

"Well, thank you but without this letter and the stamps, the family would never have had a chance to find their legacy," said Wendell.

Feeling the carriage slowing, Wendell looked out the window. "Well, here we are at Constabulary. Sorry we have to put you through this, but you are the only ones who can give us a positive identification on Edward Keith."

Constable Davis was waiting for them and in short order, they were escorted to the morgue.

"He's not a pretty sight," said Davis.

"We've probably seen worse in our lifetime, Constable," said Martha.

Davis pulled out the gurney and removed the sheet. Both women let out a small gasp. Martha spoke first. "Well hello, you bastard. Yes, unfortunately, this is our cousin Edward."

On the ride to the Duncombe farm, Wendell and Michael finished telling the sisters about Oliver's fight with Edward Keith, what they found in the mausoleum, and their own fruitless search the previous night.

"So you think there may have been someone aiding Edward?" said Lenora.

"He could never have lifted the casket out and laid it on the table by himself. It took four of us to lift it back in," said Michael.

"We may never find out for sure," said Wendell. "However, it is possible that whoever aided him may have taken the treasure, and that's why no one in the family has found it."

"If it was ever there," said Lenora. "Besides, knowing Edward Keith like we do, he would have never trusted anyone else, so I'd guess if you didn't find anything on him, it wasn't there in the first place."

"How much longer?" said Martha.

"We're almost there," Michael said. "One more turn, then we'll be on our road."

"I wonder if they've found anything this morning?" Martha asked.

What Lenora and Martha would call a farmhouse was entirely different from the house that greeted them. The parlour was decorated in Victorian style, reflecting the furnishings of a well-to-do, middle class family. There was a beautiful piano at one end, with a fireplace at the other. A huge mirror hung over the mantel and prints of Victoria and Albert and the Royal family adorned the other three walls.

Oliver and Dorothy showed them into the parlour and Dorothy served them tea on a large, oval table, upon which sat a huge Aspidistra plant.

"Everyone's at the mausoleum. Oliver will go tell them you're here," said Dorothy.

"I'll go with you Oliver," said Michael.

"They likely know we're here, Dorothy, the noise of the carriage and horses would have told them," said Oliver. He nevertheless excused himself and, left the parlour with Michael.

Oliver had been right and just as the two men went out the front door, Ruth and Evelyn came into the parlour from the kitchen. The four women took turns embracing one another and everyone started talking at the same time. Dorothy and Wendell watched and listened as the four women exchanged stories about the ocean trip, life in South Dakota, life in England, identifying Edward Keith, their children and grandchildren and eventually to their present circumstances in the search for the elder Giles Duncombe's secreted treasure.

"You haven't found anything yet?" asked Lenora.

"No," said Ruth. "Why don't we go out and join the others and you can see for yourself."

Ruth led the way out through the kitchen door and across the lawn to the mausoleum.

"Quite an imposing structure," said Martha.

"Yes, it is. Too much for my tastes," said Evelyn.

"When was it built?" said Lenora.

"In 1829," said Ruth. Prior to that, most of the relatives were buried in the cemetery, but after the flood of 1828, they built the mausoleum, and all of the recent internments are there."

"You forgot Esther," said Evelyn to Ruth, as they walked.

"Oh yes, Giles Senior's second wife is buried in France."

As they came closer to the mausoleum they could hear voices coming from inside engaged in what was obviously a heated argument.

"Well, I for one give up. It's not here."

"Come on Terrance, it has to be."

"But, we've tried every conceivable combination and still come back to either the crypt of Milton or the child, Melville."

"We have to be missing something," said a female voice.

"The thing we're missing Sister, is that the damned treasure just isn't here."

"Or someone's taken it already!"

"Maybe we can help!" said Lenora.

They were so intent on their discussion that they didn't hear the four women and Wendell's approach, and now turned to see them standing in the doorway. James was the first to speak.

"Welcome, we must be quite a sight. All at each other's throats. I'm James," he said walking over to Lenora. "I recognize you from the pictures you've sent. And you must be Martha."

The rest joined in the greeting and Lenora and Martha met the other members of the Duncombe family. Martha noticed tears in Lenora's eyes and put her arm around her.

"Tears of joy, sister?"

"Some sadness too," she said. "This would have been so great if Ben had been here."

Terrance overheard Lenora. "William, or Ben, as he was known in America, is here through you, Lenora. We all wouldn't be here if you hadn't found the letter. Let's hope all our efforts are not futile."

"Why don't you bring us up to date," said Wendell.

After dinner they all gathered in the parlour for coffee and tea.

"I hate to admit it, but I think we're at the end of the trail," said Terrance, to no one in particular.

"Lenora, Martha, you know everything we know and have seen what we've been doing in the mausoleum. Any ideas?" said Giles.

"No, I'm sorry to say I can't add anything," said Lenora. She looked at Martha who shook her head.

Wendell cleared his throat to get attention. "I'd suggest you all relax tonight and enjoy each other's company and then tomorrow we start once again from scratch and give it a final try before calling it quits," he said.

By ten, only Mary, Tyler and Lenora remained in the parlour and Lenora took the opportunity to ask a question she'd thought of earlier.

"Mary, where's your daughter Olivia?"

"She couldn't come," was all she said.

"That's too bad. I'll look forward to meeting her later. I'll always remember her letters when she was in school and the pictures and letters that she sent to my children, especially Lila when she was older."

"Yes, I remember they both liked poetry. You know, Olivia still loves poetry and even has written several poems," said Mary.

"Say, she probably would know who wrote that verse of poetry on the mausoleum wall. I sure don't recognize it."

"Which one is that, Lenora?" said Tyler.

"You know, Tyler, the one just to the right of the entry door," said Mary.

"Yes, that's it," said Lenora. "So appropriate, too, but right off hand, I sure don't remember who wrote it."

Lenora had always been one of those people who couldn't relax her mind until she answered whatever particular problem was unsolved. To try and recollect a name or place, she would start at the beginning of the alphabet and go all the way through it until something clicked. This night she lay in bed plying that routine to try to remember the name of the poem and its author. She'd been through the letters once and was on the second running when she got to the letter I and something clicked. *Yes! That's it*, she thought. *The Invictus. I remember Olivia sending that to me years ago. Who was the poet?* She was going through the alphabet again and reached the letter F when she fell asleep.

In the morning, Lenora's mind was still pondering the question of the author of *The Invictus*. She had remembered the last lines of what she recalled was the last stanza and now recited them aloud.

> *I am the master of my fate:*
> *I am the captain of my soul.*

Martha, who was in the connecting room, using the shared bathroom, overhead Lenora's recitation, and opened the door on Lenora's side.

"What was that? Talking to yourself, Lenora?" she said.

"Sorry, guess I was a little loud. I finally remembered the name of that poem."

"You mean the one that has the verse that's inscribed on the mausoleum?" Martha said.

"Yes, *The Invictus*," she said.

"I don't recall it. Who wrote it?" Martha said.

"I can't remember, but I will. What time are we due downstairs?"

"Seven for breakfast, I believe. You'd better get going. I'm done in here," Martha said.

"Thanks." *Better forget about the poem for now.*

The morning's efforts in the mausoleum proved to be as fruitless as the previous day and night. The women, with the exception of Lenora, Martha and Mary, declined to participate in the renewed search and even Tyler, Michael and Terrance were fast loosing interest. Only Giles, James, Stephen and Wendell showed much enthusiasm for the task. By mid-morning, even they were close to admitting that the treasure was not to be found.

"Well, shall we call it quits?" James said to Giles.

"I'm about ready to. We've tried and retried every possible combination," said Giles.

"Wendell, what do you think?" said Giles.

"I'm inclined to agree, but I just have that feeling we've overlooked something. Lenora, Martha, any thoughts?"

Martha didn't respond, but Lenora seemed to be in deep thought. Then she spoke.

"How about the original letter and verse from your father. Is there perhaps a clue in there we've overlooked?" she said.

"We've read and reread it. It pertains to the envelope and the postage labels, but you're welcome to give it a try yourself," said James.

"Do you have a copy with you?" said Lenora. "Mine's back in my room in the luggage."

"Here," said Giles, handing her a folded piece of paper. "You can use mine."

"Thanks. Another thing that I've been meaning to ask is why you don't involve Oliver and his sister in the search. Hasn't their family been around here for quite a long while?"

"They have, but I doubt they could contribute anything."

"You have told them about the riddle and your search, of course." said Wendell. Giles shrugged his shoulders.

"In general terms, yes, but no specifics," said Giles.

"Perhaps you should take them into your confidence. You never know what they might be able to contribute. You've nothing to lose at this point," said Wendell.

Just then Evelyn entered and told them lunch was ready.

"Fine, thanks Evelyn, we'll be right along," said Giles.

Before they went to the mausoleum that morning, Ruth took them on a tour of the house. Lenora was impressed with the shelves of books that graced the walls of the study. After lunch, she found Ruth in the kitchen with Dorothy.

"Do you mind if I look through the books in the study?" she asked.

"No, of course not. That's really Giles's room, but I'm sure he wouldn't mind."

"What are you looking for, Lenora?" Ruth asked.

"Oh, I've been trying to remember the author of the poem that's on the mausoleum wall ever since I saw it. It's driving me crazy."

"You mean *The Invictus*," said Dorothy.

"Why yes," said Lenora.

"How on earth did you know that Dorothy?" said Ruth. Then realizing she sounded like she was talking down to Dorothy, Ruth continued. "I'm sorry, I didn't mean to imply that ----."

"That's quite all right Mrs. Duncombe, I don't take offense," said Dorothy. "I asked mother about that poem years ago when I first saw it on the mausoleum."

"That's something," said Ruth. "I've been coming here for years and never thought about where that verse came from."

"Do you remember who wrote the poem?" said Lenora.

"No, but I do believe there are several books of poems in the study. Giles Senior was a lover of poems. In fact, I think I remember my mother reading that poem to me from one of his books."

"So, there's your answer, Lenora," said Ruth. Please go ahead and use the study and I'll let Giles know."

"Thank you, and thank you, Dorothy," Lenora said as she made her way to the study. They were supposed to meet in the mausoleum in a half-hour, so she quickened her pace.

The first book of poems she found was by Keats, but she was fairly sure that *The Invictus* was not his. The second book was a collection of poems, but the index did not show *The Invictus*. Next to the collection was a small book of poems by Henley, and there it was.

Henley, William Henley, now I remember she thought. *Martha and I saw one of his plays in Chester just before she left for America.*

She opened the book and turned to the poem. *Yes!* She had been right, the verse on the mausoleum wall was the third verse of the poem. Henley had written it in 1875 when he was just twenty-six years old. She could hardly wait to tell Martha.

She closed the book, tucked it under her arm and went to find her sister.

Chapter Sixteen

She found Martha with the rest of the family in the parlour.

"Lenora, glad you're here," said Mary. "We're just about ready to leave for the mausoleum. Giles and James have already left."

"Did you find what you were looking for?" asked Ruth.

"Yes, I did, thank you," she said. She walked over to Martha. "The verse is from the poem, *The Invictus*, by William Henley. Remember, Martha, we saw one of his plays in Chester."

"Henley, you say, he was one of Olivia's favorite poets," said Mary.

Stephen overheard and commented that they had studied several of Henley's stories and poems in school. "I'm sure uncle Giles will want to know, too, Henley is one of his favorites."

"He must have been the one who had the verse put on the wall," said Terrance. "Wait a minute! Henley wasn't born until the forty's. What was the date of the poem?"

""It was written in 1875," said Lenora.

"How can that be. The mausoleum was built in 1829," said Terrance.

"Let's ask Giles," Mary said.

They found Giles and James once again searching the crypt of Melville Fuller. The looks on their faces told the rest that, as previously, their search was unproductive.

"Giles, Lenora has discovered something that's quite puzzling regarding the mausoleum," said Terrance.

"Oh, and what might that be," Giles said, his tone telegraphing his frustrations.

"The verse on the outside wall to the right of the door is from a poem by William Henley ------."

"Yes, I know," Giles said, interrupting Terrance. "*The Invictus*. It's one of his best known. What's the point?"

"The point is that the poem was written in 1875," said Mary. "The mausoleum was finished in 1829, forty-six years earlier."

Terrance now had Giles's full attention and both he and James responded almost as one voice. "That can't be right."

"But it is, don't you see. There obviously was some work done in 1875. You should remember that," said Mary.

"Quite the contrary, Mary, if you remember, I was teaching at the Sorbonne in France that year. Let's see, I was there from 1874 to 1876."

"Any changes would have had to been approved by you, however, wouldn't they?" said Terrance.

"Yes, but anything like that would have been ultimately handled by John Fitzworth, Oliver's father. He oversaw the farm operation for me for years before his death."

Giles was silent for a moment. "Let's find Oliver. He should remember. He was out of school and helping his father back then."

"I'll go get him," said Wendell.

"We should have involved him a long time ago, if you ask me," said Mary. Wendell nodded as he left to find Oliver.

Wendell found Oliver in the barn wiping down one of the horses. Wendell explained the inconsistencies of the dates and their unsuccessful search using the directions in the riddle. Oliver, of course, knew they were searching the crypts and that Caine had been doing likewise, but no one had ever asked him for any help in checking out the riddle locations.

"There's something I have to get in the house. I'll meet you in the mausoleum, shortly," was all he said, as he left the barn.

"Did you find him?" James asked as Wendell entered the mausoleum.

"Yes, and he'll be here shortly. He had to go get something in the house first," said Wendell.

"So did he say anything?" Mary said.

"Not really. He just said he'd meet me back here and left," said Wendell, sounding even more frustrated.

Just then, Oliver entered. Under his arm was a long leather tube, from which he removed several rolled up sheets of paper.

"Until Mr. Eflow explained exactly what you were about, I didn't think that this would be important, and frankly, I'd forgotten about it till now. Most of you may not remember the earthquake we had here in 1874. I was just back from London and starting to help father out on the farm. It was a shocker for our area. There was minor damage to the farm, except for the mausoleum. The two columns either side of the door and the entry wall were badly cracked. The floor buckled too."

"Why wasn't I informed of this?" said Giles.

"Begging your pardon, sir, but you were," said Oliver.

"Father wrote you in Paris and explained what had happened and what was needed to repair the building. You wrote back some days later and told father to get an estimate of what was necessary and then to contact his solicitor in York to arrange for funds."

"But surely Giles would have had the final say," said Ruth.

"Oh yes ma'am. Father got the go ahead from Mr. Bently, the solicitor, about a month later. Here, I have the final drawings for renovation, the letter and the bank draft. They've been stored in the closet in the study for years."

Oliver unrolled the sheets of paper and spread the larger documents out on the marble table. He handed one of the smaller ones to Giles.

"Here, this is the approval letter you signed in 1875."

Giles studied the document. "I obviously signed this and just forgot about it. That was a long time ago."

"What about the poem?" asked Terrance.

Oliver retrieved another of the smaller pieces of paper and handed it to Giles, but before Giles even looked at it, he starting talking. "I remember now. John knew I liked Henley and suggested the verse for the wall. The poem *The Invictus* had just been published. Amazing that I'd forgotten that."

"What I just handed you was your letter suggesting the third verse," said Oliver.

"Wasn't there always something inscribed on the entry wall?" said Terrance. "I thought sure there was."

"Yes, I remember now too," said James. "It was something about having no fear of death, or fear of dying."

"It was part of a poem by the American poet, Edgar Allan Poe," said Oliver. "Your grandfather liked his poetry."

"That explains the poem," said Giles. "What about the rest? You said there was extensive damage."

Oliver flattened out the papers on the table. "Here, I can show you better than trying to explain. These are the final architectural drawings."

What the first drawing showed was that the front of the mausoleum required major repair and to accomplish this, the overall length was increased by five feet. The two forward columns were replaced, the roof strengthened and the doorway area rebuilt, which included the Henley poem verse. The second drawing showed the changes to the inside.

By extending the outside walls, several feet were gained inside and a fifth column of crypts was added.

"Another row of crypts was added!" said Giles. "I don't remember approving that change."

"You must have," said Oliver. "We wouldn't have proceeded without your approval."

"You know, that since father's death, we haven't had anyone interred in the mausoleum," said James.

"That's true," said Terrance. "Then that's the answer. We all forgot about the number of crypt columns till now. There were only four when we were young, and most important, only four when father was alive."

"I don't see your point," said Mary.

"I do," said Giles. "When father wrote the riddle, his three up and four left was referenced from the first column, which now happens to be the second."

"So that means the crypt in his riddle was Melville Fuller's," said James.

"Yes," said Giles. "Fuller's, not Milton Duncombe's."

"That at least solves the riddle location, but as we've discovered, there's nothing there anyway," said Terrance.

"Did anything else change that you know about Oliver?"

"No," said Oliver.

"Then, although we've answered many of our questions, we're right back where we started," said Giles. "Wendell, any ideas?"

"No," Wendell said.

"Lenora, did you see anything in the poem in father's letter that I gave you yesterday?" said Giles.

"Actually, I forgot about that, sorry. I got sidetracked trying to figure out the origin of the verse on the mausoleum wall," Lenora said.

"I took another look at it myself," said Terrance. "I couldn't see anything there that we didn't see before. Besides, it had to do with the postage labels."

"You can't be completely sure of that, Terrance," said Giles.

"I'll read it over again tonight, just to make sure," said Lenora. "Martha can too, and we'll have another opinion."

It was a sober and somber group that ate together at the York farm that evening. Dorothy prepared one of her specialties, rack-of-lamb, but only Michael seemed to have any appetite for the meal, asking for a second serving of lamb even before most had taken more than a few nibbles.

Even the excellent bottles of cabernet brought up from the wine cellar did little to lighten the gloomy scene. Finally, Giles rose with his glass.

"I know we are all disappointed, but there is one thing. Father wanted us to get together as a family, and we've honored that wish. Here's to father and our departed brother, William."

Jasper Fitzworth installed the massive knocker on the front door in 1849, and when employed, it left little doubt that someone was seeking entrance. The sound of the huge ring striking the metal pad now resounded through the house and interrupted their toast. Everyone was suddenly silent.

"I'll go see who it is," said Dorothy.

She could be heard opening the door and talking to the visitors. "Here, let me take your coats. My, it's great to see you and I know your mother will be happy you're here. They're all in the dining room."

Mary knew who it was in an instant and she rose to greet her daughter. Olivia, however, was not alone.

"Olivia, how wonderful." Mother and daughter embraced and Tyler also rose to welcome his daughter, but glared menacingly at the man who accompanied her.

Olivia separated from her parents and turned to the other's at the table. "Everyone, for those of you who don't know him, this is Henry Spencer."

There were few secrets in the Duncombe family and few, if any, not only knew of Henry, but knew from whence he came. Only Evelyn Duncombe, Michael, Sarah, Lenora, Martha and Stephen did not know of Terrance's long ago affair with Anne Spencer. Stephen rose first and offered his hand to Henry.

"Henry, great to see you again. It's been a while. I've missed you at the factory," he said.

"I've missed you too." Then turning to face Terrance. "You too, Mr. Duncombe."

"Quite right, Henry, good to see you again," said Terrance. "Olivia, this is your aunt Lenora, and her sister Martha O'Toole from America."

Olivia smiled broadly. "Aunt Lenora. After all these years."

"Oh, Olivia, this is great. I wish Lila was here, too."

"Yes, me too," said Olivia.

"Dorothy, bring two more chairs and two more glasses. It looks like the whole family is finally here," said Giles.

"Uncle Giles, let's remember our cousins in America, too," said Stephen.

"Quite so. No offense Lenora," Giles said. He raised his glass once more. Here's to all the Duncombes, both here and in America, to Tyler and our guests Wendell and Henry.

Henry caught Terrance's eye and winked. Then, he too raised his glass in the toast. The irony of the situation was not lost on Tyler Kirkland, and he glanced at his wife, who he noticed was staring directly at Henry.

"Have you eaten Olivia?" said Mary.

"Yes. At the train station," she said.

As the evening passed, the conversation always returned to their quest and the disheartening fact that they seemed to be at a dead end. Without any further revelations, there were only two conclusions. Some person or persons unknown had found the treasure and long departed, or their solution to the riddle was wrong and the treasure lay in another location.

Olivia and Henry listened intently and feigned surprise at most of the information, but showed genuine shock at the news of Caine's death.

"And you say this Caine fellow may have found the treasure," said Olivia.

"We doubt it, but Wendell thinks there's a chance he may have and that whoever helped him has the treasure," said Giles.

"If it was ever there," added Mary in a sarcastic tone.

Mary got up from her chair. "As for me, I'm going to bed. Tyler, are you coming?"

"In a minute. I want to spend a little more time with Olivia," he said.

"Very well, then. I'll see you all at breakfast," said Mary.

"I think we'll head upstairs too," said Giles. "Olivia, if she hasn't already, I'll see that Dorothy has prepared a bed for you and for Henry. Goodnight."

Later in her room, Lenora waited for Martha to finish with her toilet and once again read the letter with the riddle about the postage labels. *Is there something we're missing?* She mulled over each line and tried to relate it to the postage stamps and their hidden message. With the exception of the first two lines, all were clues to using the stamps. She said aloud the first two lines.

"To my beloved children I dedicate this game.

Solve the riddles, open a name, a fortune you'll claim."

Open a name. What's that got to do with the letter?, she thought. *Maybe he meant open the letter with a name. That doesn't make sense, all the envelopes had names on them.*

"I'm done, Lenora," said Martha from the bathroom.

Lenora set the letter aside. "Thanks."

As she prepared for bed her thoughts came back to that same passage. *Open a name, if not the envelope, what else?*

"Goodnight Martha, see you in the morning," she said as she blew out the candle and went to her room. Tomorrow they would be leaving. It was worth the trip even if they hadn't found the treasure. The next few days with her mother and father were far more valuable, as far as she was concerned.

Somewhere in the middle of the night it came to her. *That's it*, she almost said aloud.

She slept little the rest of the night and was up at first light. Being careful not to awaken Martha, she washed quickly, dressed and went downstairs. Only Dorothy was in the kitchen.

"Is anyone else up and about?" she asked.

"Yes, Mr. James and his wife went for a ride and Mr. Eflow is having coffee on the veranda."

"Thank you. I'll have some coffee too, and if you don't mind, I'll have it with Mr. Eflow."

"How about some toast?"

"Yes, that would be nice too."

She went out the glass doors and walked over to where Wendell sat. "Good morning."

"Good morning to you Mrs. Duncan. Please join me."

"Thank you." Then not able to hold back, she told Wendell her idea on the location of the treasure. When she finished, he, at first, said nothing. Then a smile spread across his face.

"You know, I'll bet you're right!" he said.

Dorothy arrived with Lenora's coffee and toast.

"Thank you, Dorothy," Lenora said.

"Lenora thinks she knows the answer to the riddle. What do you think of that?" Then without waiting for a response, "As the others come down, tell them to join us out here, and if you see Oliver, ask him to join us."

He turned back to Lenora. "The more I think about it, I'm sure you're right. When they're all down, we will tell them and see for ourselves."

"James has gone for a ride," she said.

"We'll wait for him too," said Wendell. "Why didn't I get that clue. I have to hand it to you Lenora, it was right there all the time and we didn't even see it. Congratulations!"

When they were all assembled, Wendell told them that Lenora had come up with a very plausible idea and to follow him to the mausoleum. Oliver was waiting for them with his toolbox. Wendell lost little time in telling them Lenora's idea.

"We've always assumed that the riddle in the original letter pertained exclusively to the envelope and postage stamps. There is one line, however, that doesn't seem to fit that pattern. Line two says, 'Save the riddles, open a name, a fortune you'll claim.' Lenora surmises, and I'm inclined to agree, that 'open a name' just might mean this."

Wendell stopped talking and taking a prying bar and a hammer from Oliver, he began to remove the metal nameplate from the thick door of the crypt of Melville Fuller. The others watched intently, as one side, then the other came free. Wendell lay down the plate and the tools and reached into the void.

"I believe these are what you've been searching for," he said as his hand came out with five cloth bags.

No one said anything. Giles took the bags from Wendell and laid them on the table. Then he loosened the drawstring on one bag and emptied the contents into his palm..

"My god."

In his hand were six brilliant stones and a folded piece of paper.

"Those are diamonds!" said James.

"I believe they are," said Giles. "Several carats each, by the looks of them. They're beautiful."

He handed a bag to James, Terrance and Mary. Then he turned to Lenora. "Here, this belongs to you."

"There's a note from father in mine," said James.

"Yes, there's one in mine too," said Terrance.

"Why don't you read yours, James. I suspect they're all the same," said Giles. And James read aloud.

Dear children,
If you are reading this it means you found the treasure
in the allotted time. I am truly glad and happy that you
worked together to solve the puzzle. I love you all
and pray that you will find a way to resolve your
differences and remain close. The diamonds are not a
reward, but a gift. Use their worth to better your lives
and the lives of future Duncombe generations.
Your father, June, 1871

"Just think, he wrote that almost 37 years ago," said Giles.

"What's disheartening though, is that if his barrister's firm hadn't burned down in 1872, we wouldn't be here and the diamonds would have been donated to charity," said Mary.

"Yes, he did take a big chance. Very risky, when you think about it," said Giles.

"Of course, he didn't anticipate William leaving either," said James.

"What do you think they're worth?" said Terrance.

"They look like they're at least two carats," said Ruth. Then taking one from Giles. "This one is beautifully cut and is very clear."

"So what does that mean?" said Terrance, repeating his question. "You're no expert."

"Still, I'd say they are valued at around 10,000 Pounds," said Ruth. "Certainly, we'll need to get an appraisal."

"Each one?" said Terrance.

"Yes, each," said Ruth. "Which means that if they're all like this one, each bag is worth around 60,000 Pounds."

"A small fortune, for sure," said Wendell. "Your father left a lot to chance and the result could have been much different, but in the end, the 'game' as he called it did bring you together and I must say, with rewarding results."

"Amen to that," said Giles.

The rest of the day, the Duncombe heirs made their individual plans. Wendell suggested that the diamonds be put in safe keeping as soon as possible and to make arrangements for them to be shipped securely to each one's own bank. For Lenora, he suggested she have the stones shipped by special courier to Barclays' Bank in London and then she could decide whether to dispose of them before returning to America.

The mood was jubilant that evening at the Duncombe farm as they enjoyed the evening meal and made their plans for departure. Lenora wanted to spend more time with Olivia before she and Martha left in the morning for Chester. Olivia had been very quiet during the meal and Lenora sensed she was troubled by something. She caught Olivia's eye as everyone was leaving the table.

"Olivia, can we spend a few minutes together? I know Lila would be disappointed if we didn't talk some more."

"Yes, I'd like that," she said and turned to tell Henry. He smiled and gave her a kiss on the cheek.

"See you later, then, dear. Goodnight, Lenora," he said and left to join the men in the study. *Hopefully Tyler and my father will act civil,* he thought.

"Let's go out on the veranda, Lenora," Olivia said.

"Yes, that would be nice."

"Let's sit here," said Olivia, with a quiver in her voice. She motioned to the two wicker chairs that faced each other in the corner.

It was obvious to Lenora that Olivia was upset about something and reached across to pat her hand. "What's the matter? You seem ill at ease. I hope I haven't made you feel uncomfortable for some reason."

"No, it's nothing you've done," she said.

"Is it something to do with Henry?"

"In a way. Well, in a big way. I'm sorry, I know you probably wanted to talk about Lila," Olivia said.

"That's true, but let's talk about what's troubling you first," Lenora said.

Slowly and with tears welling up in her eyes, Olivia unburdened her soul. She told of her teenage problems with her mother, her several failed romances and then falling in love with Henry Spencer. Then she told of the shock of learning that Henry was in fact her cousin; all about his mother Anne Spencer; Anne's relationship with Terrance Duncombe. Next she told about her parents knowledge of her relationship with Henry and their open disapproval. She then confessed about the entire scheme developed by Anne Spencer and Edward Keith, hers and Henry's involvement and their failed attempt to steal the treasure from the family. Finally she told of their plans to marry and immigrate to Canada.

"Why did you come back?" said Lenora.

"I never felt right about the whole thing and only agreed to please Henry."

"So, how does Henry feel now? He'll still not gain any of the inheritance," said Lenora.

"Actually, it was Henry who insisted we return. When he saw the real Edward Keith, it really opened his eyes and over his mother's objection, he decided to return with me and try to make our peace with my parents."

"Do you still plan to go to Canada?"

"I'm not sure now. Originally, we were all going, including his mother. I don't think she'll leave now. She planned to use some of the money for that."

"So you don't think Henry would go without his mother?"

"No. It was such a wonderful dream. To marry when we got there and make a new life where no one knew the family connection."

"Someday you may inherit money from your parents, you know," said Lenora.

"I doubt they'll put me in their will, if they find out I married Henry. Especially if we leave England," Olivia said.

"Why not come to America?" Lenora said.

"We never thought about that because Edward Keith said he had great connections in Canada."

"Keith's dead now," said Lenora.

"It's something to think about, but I'm sure Henry will not leave England now. His mother's getting on in years and we've barely enough money to pay for our own passage."

Lenora squeezed Olivia's hand. "Thanks for telling me all this."

"No, thank you. From our letters, I've always felt a connection with you and I needed to confide in someone. Now I just have to face the consequence of what we've done." Olivia bowed her head in resignation.

"I see no reason to tell anyone. You took nothing and Keith's death was none of your doing. You and Henry have a rough road ahead and why complicate it. What you've told me, stays with me." Lenora rose and pulled Olivia into her arms. "Promise me you'll think about coming to America."

"I will, and thank you Aunt Lenora."

By early afternoon the next day, only Giles and Ruth remained at the York farm. Oliver had just left for the train station with Terrance, Evelyn, Steven and Wendell Eflow. It was his third trip of the day.

"Do you think Evelyn knows about Henry?" Ruth said.

"If she does, she's never let on," Giles said.

"He looks so much like Steven," Ruth said. "What will become of them?"

"Who?"

"Olivia and Henry," Ruth said.

"Your guess is as good as mine, dear. Mary will likely never accept Henry and then of course, there's his mother Anne Spencer."

Ruth stepped closer to her husband. "Are you glad it's all over?"

"Yes, very. It's like the Duncombe farm has finally given up its secret, and father's wish for the family now has a chance to come true."

The Penny Red Enigma

Part Three

Part Three

1910

Lives of great men all remind us
We can make our lives sublime,
And, departing, leave behind us
Footprints on the sands of time.

Longfellow

Chapter Seventeen

Many a wagon axle had been broken on Main Street and this year the spring rains had deepened the ruts and enlarged the potholes, so the ride was even more fraught with potential disaster. The Mason's wagon came close to tipping over several times before Jesse finally got to the old Huffman house that served as the town hospital. He helped Lila down and offered Lenora his hand.

"No, you go ahead and get your wife inside. I'll take the wagon around back and be there shortly," Lenora said.

"All right," said Jesse and turned to follow his wife, already disappearing through the door. Once inside, he saw that Olivia had Lila in a wheelchair and was pushing her down the hallway. "Go ahead and register at the desk, the paperwork is waiting for you," Olivia said, stopping for just a moment.

Jesse's parents were one of the first families in Philip to get a telephone and Jesse had called the hospital from his folk's when Lila's labor pains became more frequent. He, Lila and Lenora came into town two days previous, so they could be close when the time came to deliver their first child.

Jesse motioned to Lenora as she entered.

"Olivia just wheeled her away," he said.

"Which way?" she said anxiously.

"Down that hallway," he said, while pointing.

"There's a new waiting room in Maternity. When you're finished, I'll meet you there," Lenora said, and went down the hall indicated by Jesse.

Just as Lenora left, Paul Blanton entered the lobby and spotted Jesse. "I got a call from your dad and got here as soon as I could. How is she?"

"She's fine. Lenora is with her," he said.

"Well, I guess you and I are relegated to the waiting room," Blanton said.

"I guess so. Lenora said she'd meet me there."

Jesse William Mason was born at 7:14 P.M. on September 9, 1910. Clarence Giles Mason was born two minutes later.

Twins were always unusual and in this case, totally unexpected. Olivia Spencer delivered the news to the waiting men and it was good that Paul Blanton was with Jesse, as the rugged rancher turned pale and unsteadily sat down when he heard the news. Henry Spencer had joined the men in the waiting room after closing the blacksmith's shop, and he patted Jesse on the back.

"Congratulations, Jesse," Henry said, and gave his wife a hug before she turned to leave.

"Thanks, Henry. You're going to be a father yourself in a month, I hear," said Jesse.

"Yes, but just one child, no twins, " he said with a laugh.

Even though Henry had been told that he was likely infertile, with the chances of birth defects, Olivia and Henry had decided not to take the risk. They put their name in for adoption at the agency in Rapid City. Just a few days ago, they got the word that a child would be available in October.

"Oh, come on, I need company," Jesse continued. Then he noticed a sad look come over Henry's face.

"If only mother was here to be a part of all this," Henry said.

"Yes, I know," said Jesse, putting his hand on Henry's arm.

Anne Spencer died the previous year. Shortly after her death Lenora and Lila received a letter from Olivia. Now that Henry's mother had passed on, there was nothing holding them in England. Two months later they were on their way. Lenora arranged for Angus Tetherton to meet them in New York and help them with their travel arrangements to Philip. Lenora also knew that their small hospital could use the help of a well-qualified nurse, so there was a job waiting for Olivia. Henry found work, too. As luck would have it, Frank Knutson was looking for someone to partner with him and open a blacksmith's shop. Lenora loaned Henry the money and now he and Frank had a thriving business.

"You're lucky to get a child so soon," said Jesse.

"Yes, Olivia was quite surprised, us being so new and all."

Olivia returned with Lenora. "Want to see your sons, Jesse?" said Olivia. "Pastor, want to tag along?"

"Yes, I'd like that."

Lenora stayed with Henry.

"It will be your turn next," she said. "I hear it's to be a boy."

"I'm still worried. We're not citizens yet," he said.

"I'm sure everything will be just fine, Henry."

"Oh look, here's Pastor Blanton, back already. That's probably why he stuck around so long, so he could sign up two new members," she said, while smiling.

"More likely to spend time with you," he said, and winked at Lenora.

"Oh, come on Henry," she said.

"What do you mean, *come on,* everybody knows he's sweet on you," Henry said.

When Henry and Olivia had first tried to adopt the previous year, they ran into several stumbling blocks. The most prominent problem was that they were not yet citizens. Over the years, Lenora and Martha's friend Teddy Roosevelt had told them if she they ever needed a favor to just write him. And so Lenora did. Roosevelt's second term as president had ended, and Lenora read he was soon leaving on a hunting expedition to Africa. She didn't expect to hear back. However, true to his word, she got a letter a few weeks later, and he promised the matter would be taken care of. A week later, Henry and Olivia got a letter from the adoption agency saying that they were now on the list and to come to Rapid City and fill out all the final forms.

That wasn't the only letter she received that week. The second was from James Duncombe. Enclosed with the letter were 210 one-penny British stamps.

Lenora,
Recently found these in some old things of father's.
They're most likely the other stamps from the sheet he used to mail the letters with the puzzle, as a sheet had 240 stamps.

These 210 One Penny Red stamps may not have any large financial value, but I thought you deserved them as a remembrance and for all your help. The family sends their love and we look forward to seeing you all at the reunion next year in York.

James

Lenora looked at the stamps sent by James. *These will make good presents for the grandchildren*, she thought. *Who knows, some day they may be worth something.*

She heard the sounds of an approaching buggy. *It couldn't be the Herrman brothers, they'd finished painting the house yesterday.*

Maybe?

She rose and looked out the window and knew she'd guessed right, and smiled to herself.

"Hello, anybody home?" he called.

"In here, Pastor Blanton."

"Don't you think it's about time you called me Paul?"

After supper, they sat close together on the sofa and reread James' letter by the light of the fire.

"Just think, Lenora, Jesse and Clarence's great-grandfather Giles, is reaching out to them after all these years."

"Yes, but not just them, all the grandchildren. It's as if his arms are still wrapped around his whole family, even extending across an ocean, molding us, and willing us to love one another."

My Harvest Song

My hands are waves and dunes
Scattering the sand and shells
They bear the wind
And break the glass
My eyes are the sun and moon
Cradle me against the tide
Rippling across the ocean
Let the sun heal the jags
Let the tide smooth the edges
Touch my heart, my children,
Lift me into the folds of silk
Wash my feet in red wine
Break bread over them. My hands
Are hills and valleys
Shaping your stories, whispers
In my ears burning cold
Lie with me, just a moment
In a bed of oak and memories
Let the earth cool your temper
Let the worms move across
My skin. My hands, my children,
Are sickle and shovel
They dig into your souls
Spades probing the holes
My fingers squeeze
Your heart, pumping, filling
Draining, pulsing
A liquid stain of ours
Pray for me, my children,
Let the cadence of psalms
Let the notes of reckoning
Be your shield and sword
Let the words cut deep
Sing my harvest song   *- Gregory Burton*

 **E**pilogue

Scott's Standard Postage Stamp Catalogue of 2004 lists a single, unused copy of Great Britain catalog number 33, plate #225, at a value of $1200.00.

The towns of Hilland, Ask Creek and Grindstone exist only in the memories of the ancestors of the early settlers, many of whom still ranch and farm the original family homesteads. Philip today is the County Seat of Haakon County, South Dakota. Haakon County was formed in 1914 from part of Stanley County.

A street in York England is named after the Duncombe family and Giles Duncombe's great grandson William operates the farm outside of York. William and his wife are planning the next family reunion at the farm, where another generation of children will participate in the traditional treasure hunt.

Other Books by Hal Burton

Cave of Secrets – 2002

A fictional tale of love, tragedy and discovery set against the background of the rugged coastline of the State of Washington's Olympic Peninsula. *Cave of Secrets* chronicles the search for the wreckage of an ancient Chinese junk that went aground with its treasure of gold coins and a priceless burial urn. A University of Washington professor uncovers the story of the junk's voyage while doing research in Taiwan. Agents of the People's Republic also learn of the discovery and set their own plan in motion to recover the treasure.

Links to the events surrounding the shipwreck in 500 AD and a mysterious disappearance in 1966 are revealed as the reader follows the search team along the coastal trails, into the caves that dot the hillsides, and to the Makah museum at the northern most tip of the United States.

Finally the reader has the answers to the secrets of the cave and the mystery of the burial urn and treasure of gold coins.